THE THREE MARIAS

THE TEXAS PAN AMERICAN SERIES

The
Three Marias

By RACHEL DE QUEIROZ

Translated by Fred P. Ellison

ILLUSTRATED BY ALDEMIR MARTINS

UNIVERSITY OF TEXAS PRESS, AUSTIN

The Texas Pan American Series is published
with the assistance of a revolving publication
fund established by the Pan American Sulphur
Company and other friends of Latin America
in Texas. Publication of this book was also assist-
ed by a grant from the Rockefeller Foundation
through the Latin American translation program of the Association of American University
Presses.

Library of Congress Catalog Card Number 63–17615

First Paperback Printing, 1985

As Três Marias was first published in
Rio de Janeiro, Brazil, in 1939 by
Livraria José Olympio Editôra.

Êste livro é dedicado ao poeta

MANUEL BANDEIRA

INTRODUCTION

THERE ARE GOOD REASONS why the present novel of
Rachel de Queiroz should be translated for the English-
language reading public, and, indeed, why she herself
should become better known in this country. Of her
four novels, none of which has hitherto been translated
into English, *As Três Marias* (*The Three Marias*, 1939)
is the most satisfying artistically; the handling of sty-
listic and technical problems is mature, and the work itself deserves its prominence in contemporary literature.
Her writings form part of a vigorous recent movement
in Brazilian literature that has produced the so-called
"novel of the Northeast." Her first novel, *O Quinze*
(*The Year Fifteen*, 1930), written before she was
twenty, was one of the early monuments of the region-
alist-traditionalist movement that got underway in the
mid-nineteen twenties. *João Miguel* (*John Michael*,
1932) and *Caminho de Pedras* (*Rocky Road*, 1937)
confirmed and extended her national reputation. *The
Three Marias* is more universal in its appeal than any
of her earlier novels, with their strong regional charac-
ter and sober social preoccupation. Representing her
newest literary trend, two highly successful plays,
Lampião, 1953, dealing with the Northeastern bandit
by that name, and *A Beata Maria do Egito* (*Blessed*

Mary of Egypt, 1957), treating a theme of religious fanaticism, have likewise had a regional flavor. In both novels and plays, however, social questions have been but a backdrop for the presentation of individual men and women of her native Ceará in their personal situations and dramas.

Because of its telluric qualities, the novel of the Northeast has attracted attention not only for its literary value but also for its interest as a kind of social document. *The Three Marias* is no exception, though it is more subtle and indirect in its presentation of a fundamental Brazilian theme, that of the status and role of woman in society, with which Rachel has been centrally concerned in most of her books. (We refer to her with the touch of informality Brazilians reserve for those in the public domain.) For the setting of *The Three Marias* the novelist calls upon her memory of early experiences in a convent school in Fortaleza, the Colégio da Imaculada Conçeicão or School of the Immaculate Conception, which she attended as a young girl in the early 1920's, graduating in 1925 at the age of fifteen. The school, which embraces all grades from preschool through what is approximately equivalent to the final year of an American high school, imparted a strongly aristocratic flavor to education. Offering the sort of refinements that would be encountered in a "finishing school" in our own country, it may be considered typical of the more distinguished among Brazilian secondary schools, 90 per cent of which are even today in private hands and require such tuition fees as to constitute one barrier to effective democratization of education at this level.

It was the translator's good fortune to be able to visit the Colégio, which is administered by the originally

French Sisters of Charity of Saint Vincent de Paul. In the company of friends of Rachel de Queiroz, it was possible to verify the considerable extent to which *The Three Marias* is an autobiographical novel, at least in many of the episodes related to life in the convent school. Maria Augusta (Guta) is identified with Rachel herself, as Maria José and Maria Glória are with two schoolmates of the author, one of whom has remained a particularly close friend to this day. Though the factual basis for the first third of the novel is strong, there is no wish to suggest that any of the episodes beyond the high convent walls are anything but fantasy. The three Marias of the title, of course, have Biblical connotations that are quite proper to the atmosphere of the convent school. A further meaning of the title concerns the three bright stars at the center of the constellation of Orion, which are better known by this name in Brazilian culture than in our own.

Except for a brief excursion to Rio de Janeiro, the scene of the novel is Fortaleza, the capital of Ceará and now a city of nearly half a million people. It is a thriving seaport and industrial center, though the colonial atmosphere persists in the older quarters. Despite the city's proximity to the equator, the inhabitants enjoy a pleasant climate with an off-shore breeze and ample rain, and striking tropical vegetation. More important than Rachel's school years in Fortaleza have been those spent in the nearby *sertão*, or arid backlands, which make up the vast majority of the lands of Ceará, the largest of the five Northeastern states comprising the so-called bulge of Brazil. Two of her major novels, both her plays, and numbers of short essaylike *crônicas* have this area as their setting. Rachel's ranching family has long been established in the country around Quixadá, some 125 miles south of Fortaleza. She remembers childhood days when bandits surrounded her father's ranch. Pilgrimages of backlands mystics and the hegiras of drought refugees were real experiences in the *sertão*. It has always been home to her, and she journeys back each "winter" (the wet season in the *sertão*, which, approximately, corresponds to the wet, cool season in northern latitudes) from Rio de Janeiro, where her professional commitments as a writer and her family obligations as the wife of a physician require her presence the rest of the year.

The *sertão* of Ceará is of such importance in the life and work of Rachel de Queiroz that it may be proper to suggest something of its nature and its contrast with the coastal area, as observed in a recent *crônica* by the novelist herself. It was written in defense of the Serra de Baturité, a highland oasis, less than a hundred miles from Fortaleza; through the possible construction of a dam to furnish hydro-electric power for the region, its lands are being threatened with inundation in the name of "progress."

Ceará is, as most people know, a semi-desert region, throughout almost its entire breadth, with the exception of a very thin strip of shoreline. It has no single permanently flowing course of water—river, stream, or creek. For six or seven months out of the year, its entire vegetation is bare of leaves, desiccated, apparently dead. (And that in the good years.) . . . From the month of July until February of the next year, livestock feeds on grass that grows wild in the pastures (it is not necessary to store the grass because there are no rains to spoil it), and on dried corn stalks from the fields. During the summer months throughout the Ceará territory—as in the other states of the so-called Drought Polygon—a kind of reverse hibernation takes place: everything dries out and will green again only in the next year, if there is a rainy season. Even the fish hibernate, or rather, wait out the summer, in the sun-baked mud of the lakes, along with the frogs and other water creatures. . . .

The point is that, in the midst of this landscape where the green lasts so little, lovely oases arise that are constantly green, perennial springs, a delightful climate: these are the *serras* or mountains. Small mountains—don't forget that everything here is on a small scale; and, among our mountains, perhaps the loveliest, the most precious, because it is near the capital, and the best known and most admired, is the Serra de Baturité. Here are the apple orchards that supply Fortaleza, its gardens, its coffee groves. For they do produce coffee, and excellent coffee, in the Serra de Baturité. . . . Everything is privileged in the mountains—its fruit has a special smell—a mountain banana smells like a flower. Ah, and the roses and the pansies from Guaramiranga! Every foot of earth there is a treasure and is cultivated affectionately, like European earth, with which it has this in common: it is good and it is scarce.

The *sertão* is also of implicit importance to *The Three Marias*, in which Maria Augusta, as well as certain other girls, reflect its presence and its influence. In dealing with the status of women in Northeastern society, the novel implies a social order that has its most traditional and conservative expression in the *sertão*, rather than in the more cosmopolitan coastal cities, where change is more accelerated and, according to sociologists, where patterns of behavior influenced by Western values are becoming more and more accepted. In the patriarchal system of the *sertão*, a wife or daughter of the *casa-grande*, or manor house, has traditionally been cloistered, subordinate to men, except of course in the rearing of children and supervision of the house. Generally speaking, a double standard of sexual morality has been the pattern for men, while a role of exemplary purity has been expected of women, whose known transgressions have often led to prostitution or other forms of social ostracism. In one way or another, all of Rachel's fictional works have shown women protagonists challenging society. Love has been their all-consuming passion, and their social situation a motive of conflict and tension. Though some of her characters have accepted their social role, others have done so with a sense of sacrifice or compromise. The school in *The Three Marias* is a microcosm in which there is a view of many of the possibilities open to women at the different social levels. It should be made clear that the avenue of freedom chosen by Maria Augusta is not to be considered a subversion of the existing patterns. She moves rather on a personal and idealistic plane. In the final episode her maternal love for her unborn child is great, but her humanitarian love for it is even greater and leads her to an action that Rachel de Queiroz knows society will condemn.

Rachel's own career represents, in its general outlines, something of a challenge to the time-honored concept of the place of women in intellectual life. She may be considered not only the leader among writers of her sex but also the representative of a new group of culturally important women in national life. Although the past has produced some valuable writers among Brazilian women, their number has been exceedingly small, at least until Rachel's own era. Since then, according to one Brazilian critic, there have been more women writers than in all the preceding four hundred years of Brazilian history. Though real evidence is lacking, the late Lúcia Miguel Pereira has inferred from a study of literary history that feminine writers were not exempt from the limitations of a cloistered life and the socially inferior status of women in general. Despite some exceptions, literary culture has been the domain of men, as the Brazilian Academy of Letters' present-day exclusion of women fully attests. Though Rachel in 1958 received that body's highest award, she is by sex not qualified to join the immortals. It is only in this century that women have been allowed access to the university level of study for the intellectual professions. Today such eminent ladies as Cecília Meireles, Henriqueta Lisboa, Gilka Machado, Dinah Silveira de Queiroz, Lúcia Miguel Pereira, Eneida de Morais, and Clarice Lispector, among others, are contributing truly important qualities to Brazilian writing. Gaining in strength is a new tendency to accord the most outstanding of women writers high national honors and, as has traditionally been the case with men, to recognize their achievements as social thinkers and as creators of aesthetic values. The prestige of Brazilian women of letters has lately made it possible for them to receive distinguished diplomatic posts, as, for example, the position of consul general held by Dora Vasconcelos in New York.

It is indicative of the new status of such writers, and of the high degree of intellectual leadership exerted by Rachel de Queiroz, that she was offered the important portfolio of the Ministry of Education and Culture in the Jânio Quadros Government being formed early in 1961. No woman thus far had ever held Cabinet rank in Brazil, and indeed such is still the case, since for reasons that may have to do with her deep sense of modesty or her equally apparent good sense—or perhaps "feminine intuition"—Rachel declined the President's invitation. But such an honor is also a sign of the degree of social change taking place in Rachel's lifetime, some of which was anticipated by the protagonists of her books. She has become a national figure for several reasons:

her novels and plays that have been attuned to the times; her interest in political questions; and her fame as a commentator on the national scene, from the columns of mass-circulation newspapers and magazines.

Her social consciousness has accompanied the awakening interest in reform and the process of change taking place so vigorously in Brazil in the 1920's and especially the 1930's, which has been described by the anthropologist Charles Wagley as "The Brazilian Revolution." Brazilian upheavals are famous for their blandness—Brazilians know how to compromise their political tensions as well as anyone—and basic changes in social structure are the result of such new forces as urbanization, educational reform, and industrialization. Like the other novelists of Brazil's Northeast, Rachel de Queiroz has recorded seismic jolts to the older patriarchal system based on large landholding and monoculture, and involving a rural and now urban proletariat emerging from slavery only in this century. Along with her concern for the role of women, Rachel has been much interested in such regional problems as the human consequences of cyclic drought in the Northeast; in the traditionalism inherent in the ancient system of feudal lords and serflike workers in the arid backlands; and especially in the problems of large-scale religious fanaticism and banditry caused by isolation and dislocation in the same area. These problems have also national implications—some of them, international—since the Western nations, particularly the United States, are concentrating a major effort of economic assistance to this same Northeast, in order to reintegrate it into the national economy and to buttress it, if possible, against the inevitable pressures toward violent leftist-inspired rebellion.

Like many other writers of Latin America, who have traditionally combined political activity with a career of letters, Rachel de Queiroz has not hesitated to engage in political activity, though it was limited, however, to a youthful involvement during the agitated early 1930's in Fortaleza. As a consequence of a brief stay in Rio de Janeiro in 1931, she joined the Communist Party but was soon expelled from it because of her Trotskyite sympathies, which she maintained until Trotsky's death in 1940. Her biographer Renard Perez tells us that because of her earlier involvement with the extreme left she was imprisoned for three months in the movie auditorium of the Firemen's Barracks in Fortaleza during the nationwide political unrest of 1937. It was in this era that her copy of the "Surrealist Manifesto," in red covers, was confiscated as a subversive document! Her political writings in recent years have denounced Stalin's betrayal of the Russian Revolution and have reflected her view that in Brazil no compromise with Communism is possible. Her own present political stand, which is mentioned merely as an example of the influential left-of-center position of many Latin American writers, is that of an "independent socialist."

The influence of Rachel de Queiroz in the cultural life of Brazil is based not only on her purely literary writing but also, especially where the great masses of readers are concerned, on a form of prose the Brazilians call the *crônica*. The best of its kind are created by masters of other literary forms, for example, Rubem Braga, Carlos Drummond de Andrade, Lêdo Ivo, Manuel Bandeira, and Fernando Sabino. Its vehicle is journalism, and therefore it is short, shorter than the essay—and rapid. Eduardo Portella has shown that the form, whose most distinguished practitioner was Machado de Assis, shares boundaries with other briefer literary forms, especially the short story and the prose poem, and that the *crónicas* of Rachel often oscillate between these several possibilities. Since the war years she has written hundreds of them; for almost ten years she has contributed a weekly brief essay, often with short-storylike or poetic qualities, to the mass-circulation magazine *O Cruzeiro*, whose last page, or "Ultima página," belongs to her. In recent years two collections of the best of her writings in this genre have been published. In these she writes in direct, colloquial style and with acute perception of human motives.

One aspect of Rachel's novels might perhaps be better understood in the light of her *crónicas:* her sincerity in coming to grips with the most fundamental of human emotions, particularly love, grief, pain. A good example is the *crónica* called simply "A Letter," written several years ago to a young girl named Aspásia, who knew she had only a year or two more to live and complained bitterly that life had cheated her. Rachel had the courage to write:

One lives because one is born, one lives to die. Don't demand anything of life, because life is not a promise. We are the ones who attribute to it our own desires in the form of expectations. And when they are not fulfilled we blame life, which, after all, never said a word about promising us anything and showed us only the harsh obligation to keep driving ahead. And if this obligation is interrupted sooner, is it not perhaps an advantage rather than a disadvantage?

In both the fictional world of her novels and plays and the real world of her *crónicas* Rachel never hesitates to take up such themes and emotions; they are important to her because they are true and basic. In *The Three Marias* love figures prominently. The emotional world of the girls approaching womanhood is shown in its true complexity and ordered by a mature mind that is not ashamed or afraid to inquire deeply into the motives of her characters. Her approach to them is in no pejorative sense "romantic" or "sentimental." Possessed of a well-developed womanly common sense and warmth, she is more nearly a realist in the tradition of a Jane Austen, an Edith Wharton, or a Pearl Buck. Incidentally, some of the works of these three authors have been among the more than forty Portuguese translations she has made from European and American literatures.

The *cronistas* are widely known figures in the intellectual life of their country; because of national circulation, their *crônicas* are much more extensively read than their published books. Furthermore, the writer in Brazil has long had a prominent role as social thinker and commentator, rather as the French *homme de lettres* has a recognized role as critic of the multiple currents of intellectual life. The extent to which Rachel is nationally recognized is illustrated by the celebration of her fiftieth birthday in 1960, in a manner both gallant and thoughtful. On or near November 17 of that year, her publisher José Olympio, issued for the first time in a single volume all of Rachel's prose fiction, including what thereupon became the fourth edition of *The Three Marias*, as a special surprise to her.

The anniversary edition, prefaced by a poem to Rachel in the style of the popular and religious *louvado*, or laudatory poem, by Manuel Bandeira, brought an immediate response from leading writers and critics, who evidently appreciated the truly Brazilian sentiment that inspired it: Octávio de Faria, Adonias Filho, Bernardo Gersen, Antônio Olinto, Walmir Ayala, An-

tônio Carlos Villaça, among others, devoted brief eval-
uative articles in the press to her work as a whole. They
focused upon several aspects: her great value as a
cronista, appreciated both by intellectuals and the general public; the harmony of her novels as a whole, but
with a progressive technical mastery culminating in
her most complete and complex novel, *The Three
Marias*; the social consciousness to be found in all her
works; the broad scope of her literary activities; her
"motherliness" as a fundamental trait, despite her having no children of her own; and the wisdom of her anal-
yses of the characters in *The Three Marias*.

A final topic, of particular concern to the translator,
is the literary style of Rachel de Queiroz. One of her
crônicas, of 1955, entitled "Letter from a Portuguese
Publisher," reflects that an unnamed publisher in Portugal had sought permission to edit her works there,
with the proviso that she agree to certain "inoffensive
alterations" in the text, having to do with the spelling,
the placing of pronouns, and the substitution of a few
terms rare, or with a different meaning, in Portugal.
Rachel's reaction was sensitive and to the point:

These wrongly placed pronouns, this language that grates
on your ear, is our language, is our normal way of speaking,
is—I hasten to say—our literary and artistic language. We
have no other, and to return to the inflexible model of the
speech of Portugal would be for us, at this late date, a ridiculous and impossible falsification.

And with characteristic modesty, Rachel felt that much
of the essence of her writing was in language:

I am not the imaginative sort of writer who composes beautiful plots, nor do I paint the picture of an era, nor am I capable of psychological profundities, nor have I ever created
anything new or important in our nation's fiction. The small

merit I may possess is in my free and easy countrywoman's way of saying things, of telling stories about what I know and what I like. And how can a *sertão* woman, with her sing-song speech, suddenly turn her language in for pure. Lisbonese?

The admirable young critic Eduardo Portella, who has examined her style, finds simplicity to be its key characteristic:

. . . simplicity, let it be understood, that does not exclude richness of movement. Hence the fact that, stylistically considered, hers is a prose of surprising possibilities. There is in Brazil today no writer who is simpler than Rachel de Queiroz. Simplicity, that is, in the sense that sensations are established directly between the artist and the reader, without complex rhetoric and in which, nevertheless, the rhythmic novelty that characterizes her syntactic structure never for a moment sacrifices clarity and harmony.

This quite original kind of simplicity may be, paradoxically, an almost untranslatable quality. Even so, the translator is hopeful that many other valuable qualities of the novelist that have been suggested may be fully appreciated in the following pages.

F.P.E.

THE THREE MARIAS

THE ENORMOUS BLUE EMBLEM of the Virgin Mary stood out against the whitewashed wall. In the center of the patio was a sweet-smelling bower of Cape jasmine, and in its cool green shade, the figure of a young girl, bare-footed, and dressed in white—Our Lady, lovely and sad.

Around the patio the classrooms were empty, silent, and closed. The sound of footsteps grew and echoed through the corridors. The rosary at the Sister's waist tinkled, heavy with medals.

And I was afraid. The Sister was old, her gaze dull, her speech colorless and hard to hear. She seemed to be made of pale paper, of starched linen like the cornette that covered her head and that fluttered like a bird with every movement of her body. She looked like a wax doll, a figurine, a saint, anything but a real person. The wrinkled doorkeeper, nothing but bones and sinew, also did not look like a human being, nor did the other Sister who silently passed by, her head lowered, with no sign of interest, no sign of a glance. Only the adolescent Virgin Mother in the bower seemed to have any girl-ishness or youthfulness; and though made of clay she seemed to be more alive and human than those other fleshly women alongside me.

Papa, pale and upset, had gone away. My godmother

had gone away. The convent parlor, where I was waiting, was at that time empty and silent; down the corridors you could barely hear something like the sound
of a hushed and distant sea.

I drew nearer to the Sister, and tried to take her by
the hand but I lacked the courage; I asked where the
noise was coming from there in the distance.

It was coming from the evening recreation just beginning on the verandas in the farthest part of the
school; and we made our way in that direction, the
Sister and I.

Along the wide verandas we met, all dressed in sailor-
blue, hundreds of young girls of every size and every
face in the world. A group of them came up to us, smiling and curious. Immediately they seemed to me hate-
ful, mocking, hostile. I drew myself closer to the Sister.
Out in the back other girls kept coming up and I could
hear their shouts:

"A new girl! A new girl!"

The Sister put her hand on my shoulder and told
me to go play with them, and to try to have fun and
make friends.

I resisted. I was more and more afraid, and I clung
resolutely to the coarse habit of the nun. "I want to go
back where my suitcase is."

I was so distraught and felt so timid in the presence
of those girls' fresh, bold faces that I could only think
of flight; and the thought of the suitcase came to me like
salvation. My dear old suitcase: the clothes that I had
helped Godmother to label and pack, piece by piece.
But the Sister laughed. Back to my suitcase? Why? Did
I need something? It was forbidden to go back to the
clothing supply room now; you could just go at certain
times, to exchange clothing.

And the girls too had some fun out of that strange desire. The suitcase, what an idea! Was I afraid they were going to steal from me?

At the Sister's refusal and with the scoffing laughter of the girls in my ears, my heart grew heavier, and a deep unhappiness which had tormented me from the first finally took complete possession of me. I missed my suitcase like a person, it was a prolongation of my home, the only bridge between my life and that new world peopled by blue dresses, by unfriendly ugly girls bubbling with derisive giggles. My hot dry eyes began filling with water and my throat began to burn. I still had the courage to insist:

"I wanted to change my shoes."

The Sister, now out of patience, once more pushed me gently into the midst of the others:

"You can't right now, my child. At night, when you go for your bedclothes, you can change. Run along."

She withdrew. I stood there, my eyes accompanying the rapid footsteps that made the pleated hem of her blue skirt swirl. I stood listening to the ring of the medals on her rosary. Then I slowly turned to face the circle of girls which kept getting bigger and bigger and closing around me; one of them, a thin dark tiny girl, asked the question for them all:

"What's your name?"

"Guta."

There was laughter behind me. What a name! What a notion! Who ever heard of a saint named Guta?

I blushed and explained right away that my name was Maria Augusta. Guta was my nickname. "What a nickname!" And they laughed right in my face.

One of them, however, took pity and said something about bad manners and lack of charity.

The interrogation kept on: Where was I from? Was my mother living? Was my father? How old was I? Just twelve? What grade would I be in?

I kept on answering with difficulty, feeling ill and ashamed.

In a little while, happily, the girls started to scatter, running to tell the others the story of the strange new girl called Guta. As they disbanded, shouting my name, they startled me more now than they had before, when they surrounded me. What made them run that way? Why did they laugh and shout?

The only one remaining with me was a thin little dark-complexioned girl, who was visibly touched by my consternation; she began to give me counsel, taking me by the arm and whispering in my ear:

"Don't worry about them, don't pay any attention. They get fun out of trying to rattle the new girls. The same thing happened to me, but I never paid any attention. Do as I did. Come take a walk."

She put her arm around my waist. I shrank back a bit, because she, after all, was not much different from the others. She too was dressed in blue, liked to ask questions, and acted superior and self-sufficient. Finally I began walking and listening to what she had to say and looking at the things she pointed out.

On the verandas where we played the lights were burning, but in the great tree-filled patios the shadows were engulfing everything, and there the Colégio seemed sadder still and more unfriendly.

Arm in arm the girls passed us by in groups, singing sad waltzes and the happier melodies of serenades. Under certain lights other groups gathered, listening to stories which one of the girls read out loud, in a moving, declaiming voice. Under other lights girls

were playing jackstones; the rock would go up in the air and then come down, and they would all crowd around with heads together as if hypnotized. Suddenly one of the players would stop, the scorekeeper would write a figure in chalk on the mosaic sidewalk, and to the shouts of "She did it! She did it!" everyone would furiously start trying to outdo her.

My friend, Maria José, took me in charge, heading for the far end of the veranda over in the distance.

She said she was going to introduce me to a girl friend, the only one "among all those hypocrites and liars I can call my friend in this school." "I'm going to show you all those I can't stand."

And she pointed out here and there her principal enemies, whom I never learned to distinguish, since I lumped them all together in my own fears: they all seemed to me so alike in their uniforms and their appearance.

"Her only friend" was seated on the ground in one of the noisy circles of players. She must have been a champion, judging from the throngs and the enthusiastic rooters. Maria José waited for her to finish, and then called her from afar with a wave.

Then she introduced me to her friend Glória, who also found my name strange and had me repeat my true name, and listened to me gravely explain that it had been I myself, when a tiny child, unable to say my own name correctly—

Glória had large eyes, was tall and thin, and bit her fingernails. She interrupted the confused ending of my explanation in which I was becoming all mixed up:

"When I heard all the shouting, I could tell it was a new girl."

I said nothing, displeased with that name "new girl," repeated so harshly, so abruptly, that it seemed an insult.

Suddenly a bell rang, loud like a church bell, and nearby, quite nearby. It startled me. Glória explained that it was the bell for evening prayers, the chapel bell. She left us, went back where she had been to join the others, and started picking up her jackstones.

At the end of the veranda, the chapel "formation" was beginning to line up, little by little and in poor order. The big girls in front, then the middle-sized ones, and the little ones bringing up the rear, noisy, disheveled, and inattentive to the sound of the Sister's clack, which sounded like a child's wooden noisemaker. The girls would run from one row to another, count up the rocks in their pockets, get in scuffles, and stifle their laughter.

Enveloped in shadows, barely illuminated by the great star-crowned figure of Our Lady on the high altar, the chapel was the fitting setting in which to give more force to the complex impression of fear, strangeness, newness, and to the imprecise feeling of anguish, which possessed me from the moment I first set foot inside this school.

I did not pray, for I did not know what they were saying. And when they came to something I did know, the Ave Marias at the end, I was ashamed to join my voice with the others', although Maria José prodded me with her elbow and made signs to me with her head.

When the table was set for tea my throat felt so tight that I could scarcely eat. As night came on I felt more and more sad and lost and everything seemed confused; nor did I feel any happier when at last I could go to the clothing supply room to get my sheets and nightgown and exchange my shoes. I felt better about things only when I raised the lid of my suitcase and the familiar, beloved smell of basil arose from the midst of my clothing. But I didn't even have time to go through any of my things or look once more at the embroidered monogram of my bedspread, which was the pride of all my belongings and which I never tired of seeing. The supply-room keeper called to me from the doorway in a strident voice: "Come along, dearie!" And I closed the suitcase hastily and set off running to the formation.

When all was quiet and I was in bed, far from Glória, far from Maria José, between two other girls even less known to me, my sorrow finally burst, and I wept and wept until I had spent all my sobs, all my tears; prostrate and exhausted, my aching head tossing restlessly on the hot hard pillow, I wept until I fell asleep.

Glória used to wear on her bosom a locket pin with two frames. On one side, the picture of a lovely smiling young girl; on the other, a man with large sad eyes and with dark hair that fell in ringlets over a wide fore-head. Two portraits of the dead, for Glória was an orphan.

And at the Colégio, among so many others who had no father or who had no mother, Glória's orphanhood became invested with I don't know what subtle characteristics which made it seem exceptional—as with a kind of tragic aristocracy. She had a guardian. At times she would say "my guardian," raising her voice importantly, and many of us would look at her with envy, and she would look upon us with disdain from the height of her drama, overwhelming everyone with her romantic childhood.

On the day of her birth her mother had died. She had died at the age of sixteen without having had the leisure to know the joys of this world, knowing of love only the suffering of its early time and of maternity only the pain and drama of childbirth.

Her husband was left lonely, heartsick, completely unsure of what to do with that little girl in his arms. She was raised without knowing mother's milk. But this was the only element of maternal care that she lacked. Her father was all things to Glória, compensating for all the tenderness that had been buried, taking the dead woman's place, as if he expected that some day she should return and take back her place. He acted like a solitary card player who, to bring illusions to his isolation, plays alternately for himself and for an imaginary opponent, inventing a presence to populate the solitude.

Until she was four, Glória called him "Mama." And the first time that she ever called him "Papa," driven to this by little neighborhood playmates who tormented her ("She's so silly she calls a man Mama!"), he wept the whole day long, and it was as if his wife had died all over again.

That's the way the three of them lived until she was twelve—the father, the little girl, and the dead wife. Standing next to the large crepe-shrouded portrait, the very one found in miniature in the locket, they used to have photographs made. Or at her tomb, with him leaning on the cross, somber of face and inconsolable, the little tot grief-stricken, dressed in white and seated on the marble steps.

The father wrote verses. Glória had a strongbox of fragrant wood with dull silver inlays in each corner which was full of sonnets and ballads, newspaper clippings, and yellowed manuscripts. Verses to his dead wife, verses of nostalgic longing and indignant grief. There were other kinds of verses too; happy or emotional ones lyrically accompanying his daughter's childhood, her first smile, her first tooth, her first step. Little rhymes which, when she was eight, Glória must have recited at school celebrations, with her little hand pointing up to heaven, "where her sweet Mama was waiting for her." She had a picture of herself thus, gravely pointing to the ceiling with uplifted eyes as she stood beside the painting of her Mama.

One day her father died. The mysterious existence made up of love and longing and shared by all three —himself, the little one, and the dead wife—was over. There were no more long walks to the cemetery in the softness of evening, when the stephanotis on the young woman's grave would scatter its fragrance among the other tombs and guide the steps of the father and the daughter who walked arm in arm. There were no more verses, gifts, nickels that she would take from his pocket when he came in from the street, no more arithmetic lessons at the blackboard nailed to the wall of his office. By then he was expecting from the girl the knowledge of a high school student; afterward he would be radiant, unable to hide his pride and joy when he saw her extract a cube root.

He died, but though dead, he left an extensive machinery of protection and assistance organized around Glória. The guardian had been named, all wealth converted into securities, a letter written to the Mother Superior of the school asking protection and love for the orphan. That well-written, pathetic, tear-filled letter was one of the legends of the Colégio and was kept in the Mother Superior's strongbox, guarded like a relic, to be given to the girl on the day of her majority.

It was told that Glória came to the school all dressed in black, her straight hair falling to her shoulders, the great locket shining on her bosom against the dark of her mourning clothes, her violin case under her arm. Because she did actually have a violin to complete the picture, she was truly *the* orphan, pale, skinny, leaning on the doorpost of the entry into the parlor, as if she had stepped out of an illustration of one of those novels that we used to read aloud at evening recreation— novels whose beginnings are so sad, but which always end with the marriage of the little orphan to the haughty young man, with laughing and scoffing steel-blue eyes, the castellan's son at the castle where she is a tutor.

And, from the day of her arrival, Glória never ceased being, for the entire school, the orphan, irremediably unhappy and inconsolable. No one was surprised to see her weeping, when everyone else was gay. Naturally, she had no father or mother. Perhaps we might even have missed it if she had not wept, and Glória herself might have been ashamed if from time to time no tears came to her. But her tears came, easily, because she was so alone and sensitive, and so desperately missed her dead father and his lost love. On the day she was fifteen, we filled her desk drawer with roses, brashly stolen from Sister Jeanne's garden. And Glória, who had come into class conversing and smiling, broke into tears when she opened her desk, thinking back on her father and other birthdays. And not one of us felt grieved nor did anyone wonder at her weeping; it was as if that were the proper ritual of the moment.

Only in her tears, however, and in her nostalgic longing, only in her black dress and sadly moaning violin did Glória represent the true orphan; she was neither humble nor gentle like other orphan girls, those found in novels. She would not win the youth with the steel-blue eyes, the aviator or lord of a castle, through any naïve gentleness. She was imperious and authoritarian; I quickly fell under her sway. I obeyed her and let myself be dominated by her in my inattentive and disorderly existence. It was Glória who handed me my hair ribbon in the morning, who put my desk in order, berating or reproving me because my notebook had no cover and my pen had disappeared.

We took the same courses and sat together.

Maria José was further up front, next to Jandira, a dark-skinned girl with violent eyes, long face, and bold spirit. We were very fond of Jandira, although in her desire to make good grades and "to sacrifice to the golden calf," as we used to say, she studied too much and was the second-ranking in the class. She was gay, high-spirited, and intelligent, knew how to recite French, and had already distinguished herself in a program at the end of the year, declaiming *Le Mort de Jeanne d'Arc* and wearing a harlequin costume.

However, despite her prominence and her distinction in the examinations, and other frivolous vanities that we looked down upon, she did have some secret affinities with us. She was a contributor to our newspaper, the *Blessed Bird Cage*, "a satirical and independent weekly," hand-printed in purple ink and illustrated in colored pencil. In one corner were the stars of the three Marias. The paper was almost entirely in verse, for destructive literature prefers the concise molds of poetry; and though defunct after the third number, the newspaper left us a taste for satire, a love for ironical illusions, for parodies and epigrams. Hither and thither between Maria José's row and our own, was a continuous traffic of little notes written in decasyllables or in sonnet form, burlesque paraphrases of "The Doves," "The Three Sisters," or "The Secret Evil." Our principal targets were the teachers, for they were the principal stars of our society; their habits, their peculiarities, their foibles, love affairs, marriages, misfortunes, anniversaries—we knew them as intimately as the English populace is said to know the peculiarities of the Royal Family: passionately and minutely.

We discovered one day, for example, that the first-ranking girl in the class was violently in love with the history teacher, a sentimental bachelor of gentle and contemplative soul. Of historical characters he preferred to admire the queens in their chambers, praying or flirting, rather than to accompany the kings in their battles and fanfare. He adored the Empress Leopoldina, Marie Antoinette, and Inês de Castro. And, perhaps because of this passion and other absurd analogies, we used to call him "Dom Pedro," and his admirer "the damsel Dona Inês."

And how intangible and pure were Dom Pedro and Dona Inês! When he asked her a question, we could see the ruler with which he toyed tremble in his hands; and she blanched, white and tremulous, like the lilies on the banks of the Mondego when the wind rocks them.

But with true heroism, Dona Inês controlled herself and recited her answer with stammering haste, while Dom Pedro listened to her, his eyes half closed with emotion.

She would stop speaking, finally, exhausting the question and her breath simultaneously, and in his small fine hand, he would lovingly write a grade in his notebook, always an "excellent."

There would then be a pause, the climax over. The professor would look for a new name in his book and we would breathe once more and look around at each other smiling and beaming at such scandalous goings on.

Dona Inês, her head lowered, absorbed and embarrassed, looked at no one else for the rest of that day.

The Colégio, enclosed in high walls, was as large as a citadel. Inside were square patios, white paths among pitanga shrubs, the Moorish quietude of a cloister.

On one side we resident students lived, noisy and very much at home, studying with professors from outside, playing the piano, and wearing our silk and white-flannel uniforms.

In the center was the "Sisters' area," great, bright, silent rooms which we never entered. And further on, built around other patios and sheltering other antipodal lives, were the houses of the Orphanage, where silent young girls, dressed in humble checks, were learning to work, to sew, to make lace for the bridal trousseaus that we should later wear, embroidering baby clothes for the children that we should have, because they were the poor of the earth and were properly learning to live and to suffer like the poor.

A traditional prohibition, based upon remote and complex reasons, separated us from them. We saw them only in the chapel, lined up on their benches on the other side of the aisle, nice and quiet and with lowered gaze, because their rules requiring modesty, humility, and silence were even more severe than ours.

And they seemed to come from everywhere—little Negro girls with round heads and furtive gaze, white girls with a sickly cast, raised in the filthy, ill-ventilated huts along river beds, country girls with Indian features from the *sertão*, some tiny and frightened, others now grown to womanhood, with straight hair and the measured gestures of a nun.

Opposite me, on the end of the bench, there was always a little freckle-faced girl, with red hair, who was like a burning light in the midst of all those discolored children. The checkered uniform which enshrouded the others never managed to suffocate her. In chapel she did not pray, she laughed to herself, laughed at the priest, laughed at the dragon which the archangel Saint Michael ran through with his lance, dropped the book they gave her to read, and shook her flaming tousled hair in the air like a firebrand.

We knew her story; her father had killed her mother in a jealous fury and was finishing up his life in the Icó jail. His daughter did not know him and spoke of him as of a stranger. And one needed only to ask and she would retell the bloody death of her mother, acting out the dramatic scene while the circle of young girls, all around, listened to her with terrified hearts, and a look-out, ten paces beyond, watched to see that no Sister was coming.

"Mama was in her hammock, holding me in her lap and giving me her breast. He came in with the letter in his hand, shoved the paper in her face, asking whether she recognized the handwriting. The poor thing didn't say anything and hung on to me without the courage to look him in the eye. And that horrible man buried the knife in her back, she gave a low moan, gradually let me slip out of her arms, I hit the floor and got all soaked with blood that was beginning to make a pool on the brick floor. He knifed her three times. She died all alone, with no one to help her, not even a candle in her hand."

I could never look at her, during mass, without her story's coming to mind. And it always seemed to me that she had some part in the crime because of her invincible gaiety, her bold eyes, her smiling white teeth. And I could see vestiges of blood spots, the blood of the dead woman, in her red hair, in her white freckled face.

Next to her sat Hosana, Maria José's friend. Those illegal and persecuted friendships with the orphans were the elegant vice, the height of sentimental refinement in the school.

Every once in a great while, by chance or prearrangement, the two would meet somewhere on a veranda, on one of the connecting sidewalks, and exchange a few startled words, like criminal lovers.

Hosana was a sickly, weak, blond girl. She embroidered beautiful things with those skinny, long, needle-pierced fingers.

An emotional relationship had been established between the two of them and had lasted a year now. They exchanged little figurines of saints worked in rich lace which cost Maria José weeks of savings and which the orphan girl, for her part, managed no one knows how. For the verse to accompany the saints they would write lyrical and glowing tributes: "The roses which you see at Jesus' feet are not so pure as your heart." "My friendship for you is like a sanctuary guarded by angels." "In your prayers to the sweet Jesus, say a prayer for one who is your friend until death."

In her prayer book, along with a saint from her first communion and a relic from Lourdes, Maria José kept a little silken square embroidered by Hosana: the names of both girls plus the words "Eternal Friendship," inside a panel of forget-me-nots. It was a treasure, admired and envied by the whole school, a treasure which Maria José showed to only a few select friends; and she never closed the book without kissing it devotedly.

And, of course, the whole excessive outpouring of romantic affection, the little flowers, the saints—everything at last got back to Sister Germana's ears, and that was always the end of any friendship with an orphan girl.

Maria José was called unexpectedly and mysteriously to the Mother Superior's office, like a conspirator caught suddenly in the midst of his bombs.

Glória and I stood by the office door listening. We heard our friend sobbing, we heard the Mother Superior call her *petite peste, mauvaise tête*.

Finally Maria José came out, with swollen eyes and heavy footsteps, her look uncompromising. She had not given in. While the Mother Superior was rebuking her, she was asking her guardian angel to protect her and not let her be false to her friend. She seemed to be able to see Hosana's blue-green eyes weeping, suffering her punishment with patience. She remembered how her fingers worked and worked, pricked by the needle, her sad anemic smile—and she resisted the Mother Superior, lowered her head obstinately, renounced nothing and didn't ask for pardon.

A few days later a note full of tearful good-byes came from Hosana. She was going away, to Baturité, to embroider the trousseau of a rich bride-to-be.

From there she sent a few letters, not saying much, with the same expressions and invocations of the dear saints of an earlier day; in the corners she wrote, "I shall miss you always! ! !" Those letters had been brought by an extern.

She met a widower, a client of the wealthy family, who was poor, miserable, and laden with children. She married him. Maria José gradually forgot her.

We later learned that she died in childbirth.

As on my first day, the Sisters always made me afraid. I would never know how to be at ease with them, or discuss and ask for things as did Glória. And, much less, like Maria José, be able to choose a friend from among the Sisters, and take her as a counselor and confidante.

And I was pained by my inhibition; but the Sisters were so distant, so different! It would have been impossible for me to discover between myself and them any points of identification, as did Maria José and Glória. I considered them outside of humanity, I had never given up the impression of supernatural distance that they had given me the night of my arrival.

I had never been able to imagine a Sister eating, getting dressed, sleeping; I could never believe that there was a woman's heart, a woman's body, beneath the heavy wool of the habit. One day, while looking at a very new Sister who had just recently come from the Mother House, I noticed her round full bosom pushing up the hard lines of her bodice. I lowered my eyes in embarrassment and confusion. That went against my personal taboos and overmodest prejudices. It was as if I had seen a profane painting upon an altar, some frivolous and sinful object where should have been a saint. All this, just because a humble bosom was asserting itself, innocent and round, where I thought should be found the sunken breast of an ascetic.

Could those womanly attributes be proper to a nun? Or then was a Sister permitted to have a bosom, to have a body, to have any beauty other than that of her hands and her face, to be lovely like any other young girl? To be lovely, for example, like the pretty sister of that Syrian school girl who had visited us the other day and had such a striking figure, or, at least to have a form such as the big girls of the Colégio already had?

Another time, during Sunday recreation, I was sitting on a step reading a novel. A young Sister, who was also new to the House, came up to me, softly, and read the title of the book over my shoulder. I turned red, with confusion, and stood up waiting for her reproving look. The Sister, however, took the volume from me, smiled, and exclaimed:

"Don't be angry, Guta, but I'm the one who is going to read it now!"

She left with the novel, sat down in the piano room, and spent the rest of the afternoon engrossed in the adventures of Magali.

Dear Sister, if you had only guessed how you scandalized my heart with its many prejudices! You did not know that I was all too human and that I considered myself weaker and more sinful than anybody else. That is why I admired heroic virtues and spent my time dreaming of impossible saints, saints made entirely of crystal and light, like a diamond. I dreamt of those ascetics from the desert who were torn by misery and by ecstasy, who pushed aside as a diabolical temptation the vision of a little brown loaf of bread in the corner of a hearth. How could I understand a nun's interests in those worldly dramas, and those profane love affairs? Why did the Sister read and become interested in the history of the love life, the kisses, and the dreams of

Magali? How could there be, beneath that habit, anything but the harsh notion of discipline, prayers, sacred history, and arithmetic problems?

For the longest time, that question bothered me, at night. What were, after all, the obligations of the habit? In my opinion, in my state of exaltation, it meant to die, to give one's blood, to destroy one's dreams, to trample one's desires, to make one's life a transparent and tortured host to be placed on the altar. I thought that a nun's heart must be old, a thousand years old. And the young Sister's was an ingenuous heart of twenty years, ignorant of the world. It was I who was wrong, I who was sinning. I who had invented the transgression and was scandalized at the innocence of that young girl dressed as a nun.

Children are as ferocious, heartless, and unbending as savages. They understand and love innocence less than anyone. I who was fourteen years old did not understand it; and it seems to me that innocence, simplicity, are refinements of souls that are already much advanced along the road to perfection.

I spoke about a book. The fact is we used to read a great deal in those days. It was precisely at that time that I discovered literature.

Until that time I had already been reading, of course, but reading like a child, for the pleasure of heroic adventures, for the marvels it suggested: Gulliver, Robinson, Captain Nemo.

In this new phase I began reading like an adolescent, almost like a woman, which I was fast becoming. I began to like books that spoke of love, the eternally roseate little French novels in which witty, bored men, fed up with sirens and with paradoxes, fell madly in love with simple girls of sixteen.

And poetry, great and divine poetry!

But now, I say with old Rousseau: it is best not to lie. Poetry enveloped me, made off with me, throttled me, it is true. But in its most banal and inferior form—in sentimental little sonnets, in inconsequential and trivial poems of love.

Any kind of facile verse by a boudoir poet, who said charming, romantic things, was sufficient to fill my eyes with tears. Oh, *Toi et Moi!* Oh, Géraldy!

Poetry, true powerful great poetry, was slowly possessing me, as my soul was gradually losing the successive layers which covered it. How many years did I not spend, how much of my soul did I not waste in second-rate emotion, until I became capable of understanding and feeling personally the beauty of *Daughter of the King?*

But, at that curious age, one is interested and moved only by the false, the artificial.

And does the lovely heroine engage in a tongue-in-cheek dialogue with a young sportsman, an Apollo with oars, a Tarzan in flannel trousers? This is beautiful and one comments upon it and learns it by heart.

But a great outburst of human passion, of pain or love, shocks and scandalizes, reveals things that people don't wish to see, a nakedness that seems to us obscene.

Any one of us would have exchanged all of Shakespeare (including Romeo and Juliet) for a single volume of *La Passagère* or of *Mon Oncle et Mon Curé*.

On a certain occasion, a volume of *All Quiet on the Western Front* happened to fall into our hands. The thoughtless brother of one of the externs left the book within her reach; she leafed through it aimlessly, saw certain scenes, brought the book to school. And it caused us only revulsion and terror.

We only understood war that had handsome heroes, dressed in sky blue, returning slightly disfigured and covered with medals to the arms of their loved ones. The other filthy unpoetic war, the latrines, the cursing, the soldiers' fear and misery gave us only indignation and nausea.

Nor was the Sisters' censure necessary to expose the book and condemn it. We ourselves banned it; and if it did linger there a while, it was in the hands of some more corrupt or curious youngster, desirous of reading about the immoralities of the soldiers with the French women, or of learning the filthy "cuss words" of the trenches.

In disapproval, we all turned to *Fiancée d'Avril*, to cleanse our souls.

It was our teacher, Sister Germana, who suggested our nickname, for the first time calling us "the three Marias."

It happened during an afternoon study period, and while everyone was reading or writing exercises in their notebooks, Maria José, Glória, and I sat in the back of the room conversing secretively.

Sister Germana suddenly came in, sounded the clack sharply:

"Maria José, Maria Augusta, Maria Glória, why don't you keep still? You three are inseparable! Have you ever noticed, girls? Those three spend all their time together chatting, idling, avoiding everyone else. They are the three Marias. A fine thing, the Lord knows, if they only lived together like the three in the Gospel! But I'll wager they're frittering away their time in dissipation."

Glória looked at me, I looked at Maria José. We smiled. "The Three Marias!" The three Biblical Marias? The three heavenly stars?

The class found this amusing and the nickname stuck. We ourselves took pride in it, we felt ourselves to be set apart in an aristocratic and celestial trinity, in the midst of all the other plebeians. Heavenly personages have a prestige that has always dazzled humans; and comparing us to the stars was like an intoxication newly experienced, a pretext for fantasies and whimsy. We loftily adopted the device. In our books, in our notebooks, a drawing of three stars together was our symbol: the three Marias of the heavens.

At night we would stay out on the patio gazing at our stars, identifying ourselves with them. Glória was the first star, dazzling and close. Maria José chose the one on the other extremity, tiny and twinkling. To my lot fell the middle one, perhaps the nicest of all; a serene star of bluish light, that undoubtedly was some tranquil sun warming distant worlds, happy worlds, that I could only imagine to be nocturnal and moonlike.

Maria José was the one who thought up the idea of tattooing ourselves. It had to be on the thigh, so that the Sisters wouldn't see. For our tastes it should have been on the arms, the neck, the shoulders; but it was necessary to avoid having the nuns find out, or having some counselor run tattle to Sister Germana.

Hidden out behind the lavatories—our regular headquarters—sitting on the ground, with our stockings pulled down, we used the point of a scissors to make the row of three stars on our thighs.

It was painful. It was done with light scraping, until the blood came. I made my cut decisively, with my teeth clenched. Glória, fainthearted and patient, made her scratches very, very slowly. And Maria José lost her courage on the last star, and it was necessary for Glória to come help her with her soft hand. From time to time she would make a face and groan, and Glória would raise her hand:

"Do you want me to stop?"

She shook her head. She had to keep going until the end. And I recalled, when my own insignia was finished, that you could fill the stars with ink and they would never fade away. I had read some place (I don't know where) that the Japanese put ink inside a tattoo right away.

Glória, who was afraid of germs and who always kept a bottle of iodine in her desk, was opposed and said apprehensively, "Who knows what ink is made of? It might be something filthy, and cause infection, tetanus, gangrene."

"You're crazy, Glória. Ink is made out of the sap of plants."

"It's also made with Prussian blue. Who can say

that it's not the same as prussic acid, the worst poison in the world?"

I quit the discussion, engrossed in contemplating my own tattoo, without looking at the others'. Red with blood, the three stars shone on my white skin as if they had flowered from the flesh.

My folks lived in the *sertão*, in the Cariri region. On that account I spent only the major holidays at home; I had the rest of the year at school: Holy Week, the Feast of St. John, the whole business.

Of the three of us only Maria José had her family and home nearby: a big country place full of small children, and with cattle all around, located at the end of the Alagadiço streetcar line.

Her father lived away and Dona Júlia, her fat and careworn mother, looked after everything. At the school there was a complicated story about their separation, with another woman mixed up in the case—a young unmarried girl who had been the youngest child's godmother, and who was treated in that home like a part of the family. Now she was living with Dona Júlia's husband in a chalet in the best part of town. Maria José herself gave us the details one day. She told us how she had come back from a Sunday outing to find her parents fighting. After that her father deserted the home and didn't even go there to sleep, and her mother was left all alone in the bedroom, occupying the big bed and holding her smallest child in her arms.

At times Maria José got permission from the Sister Superior for the three of us to spend Sunday at her house.

The truth is that the outing wasn't much fun: the big old house was uncomfortable, the grounds treeless, with only a swampy pasture, a barnyard, and a banana grove in the back; the sulky children kept disappearing; Dona Júlia was always ill-humored, eternally complaining of her absent husband, her impossible children, the thieving milkmen! There was no movie, no avenue, nothing. Alagadiço was far away and Dona Júlia was rigorous. You contented yourself with the chapel at the end of the streetcar line, where only country girls and poor folks went. Only once in four Sundays did a cadet from military school ever show up there.

But, anyway, we were eager to have those outings: they were like an escape for us and opened up the possibility of an adventure. Only rarely, once or twice every three months, did the Sister Superior ever let us go. Nor did Dona Júlia insist greatly upon it.

So on Saturdays we would put our hair up in papers, and just before leaving, add a touch of rouge disguised beneath a layer of powder. Glória, who was tall and thin, made a fetish of being slender and cinched up her waist incredibly tight. As for me, my vanity was to show off my legs. I had a horror of our uniform with its long skirts, and I spent a lot of time secretly raising the hem and paying no attention to the protests of Maria José and Glória, who called me immoral. Short skirts

made me like the elegant children from outside whose
mothers picked out their dresses for them. And I used
to come back at them:

"Only little girls who have no mother go around in
long skirts. You two look like you've just come out of
the Orphanage."

It was Dona Júlia who always came to get us, very
unpretentiously, her hair gathered into a smooth bun,
in an old made-over dress of straw-colored silk with an
embroidered red collar.

In her heart Maria José was embarrassed not to have
an elegant mother like some of the girls; she was
ashamed of that eternal dress of hers with the faded embroidery, those shoes with run-down heels that her
mother wore. And she liked it better when Dona Júlia
couldn't come and sent the maid. No one notices a maid.
Nobody should say, as one of the girls once shouted in
the middle of play period:

"Maria José's mother looks like a midwife!"

How that hurt her, how the poor thing cried in
humiliation! As if her mother were to blame. A midwife has no special kind of face, the job does not make
a person's face look different. The mother of the girl
who made this remark was a wrinkled old hussy with a
lot of grandchildren. You wondered if she ever had to
work to bring up four children, get up at dawn in the
dark to keep track of the milk, go around in clogs all
day long through the weeds and manure, whipping
the children and hollering at the milkmen!

Dona Júlia always used to say, self-pityingly:

"I've always had the luck of a no-good, thieving, runaway slave, good for nothing but a beating. Just look
at my sisters now. One of them married an army doctor
and lives in Rio; the other one's husband works for the

postal service. Neither one ever dreamed of going through what I go through!"

And she would set up on her lap the child that happened to be nearest, stroke his hair thoughtfully, and conclude:

"I wonder if when this little fellow grows up he'll ever repay me for what I've suffered for him—Let me tell you that it was all for their sakes."

The night before exams inspired collective terror, like the threat of plague in a village, accompanied as it was by its cortege of prayers, invocations, exorcisms.

Each girl stuck close to her notebooks, spent her days walking up and down the recreation area, alternately reading out loud and praying, making the most outlandish promises: to spend a month and a day sleeping without a pillow, two weeks without eating candied brown sugar, to say twenty-eight rosaries for the souls in Purgatory, or to Saint José Cupertino, the protector of students.

During those periods Jandira would go off and leave us to join the girls at the head of the class who spent their time in review sessions, where they shone in advance, discussed their grades, divided up the honors.

Among us, the reactions were different. Of the three, Maria José was the one who made the most promises. Glória, who was proud, asked nothing of the saints, and studied and studied and learned it all. I, who

studied little beforehand, always wasted my time thinking and dreaming. Only on the eve of exams did I
buckle down to the learning at hand, feverishly, hastily,
the victim of last-minute woes, running to borrow
sacred medals from the Sisters.

On the day of the biology exam, which was the worst
of all, Maria José remembered a story that Sister Germana had told: that formerly the girls used to place a
note with the name of the topic to be learned at the
feet of Our Lady in the chapel tower.

This was a way out of our troubles. On a piece of
paper we wrote: "circulatory system," and I was en-
charged to deliver it.

It was about time for the *Angelus*, and I went and
sat down, notebook in hand, on the steps of the entrance
to the chapel. Esperança, the custodian, who was going
to ring the noonday bell, passed me as she was leaving
Sister Jeanne's garden. She smiled at me, mentioned
the exams, and offered to say a novena for me. I accepted the novena and mumbled that there was still
something else I wanted besides that. I was Esperança's
favorite; I used to tell her stories, listen to her complaints, and have aspirin bought by the externs for her
headaches.

It was she who gave me the right to come and read
in the environs of the chapel, a solitary, prohibited area
that always smelled of roses from the saints' gardens.

Seeing Esperança start up the steps, I stood up,
stopped her, and drew her into a corner:

"Won't you listen to what I need to ask you, Esperança? Aren't you interested in me any more?"

And I told the story of the exam, of how afraid we
were, and of the promises that we had made. How Sister
Germana herself had said that formerly, the girls used

to go up carrying a slip of paper—I put both hands on her shoulders:

"Let me go, Esperança—You don't want us to flunk the exam and go away, leave the Colégio and never come back!"

Esperança's fat old face broke into a protesting smile, but she still told me that this was forbidden, that Sister Jeanne would never permit it if she learned about it—

"Why didn't you ask Sister Germana?"

"When, Esperança, when?"

Where was I going to find Sister Germana at that hour? The exam was to be at 1:00, and we were supposed to line up at 12:30, and Sister Germana was over at the Orphanage. I wheedled, begged, whimpered.

Esperança went up the chapel steps and looked to see that there was no Sister at prayers. Then she motioned to me:

"Go ahead."

I ascended the tower stairsteps trembling with excitement, feeling myself to be in the mysterious atmosphere of an ancient tale with that rising staircase, uncoiling like a snake within the tower, and my footsteps resounding throughout the nave (Quentin Durward, D'Artagnan, Esmeralda—).

With no show of interest, Esperanca accompanied me, panting and complaining that she had to climb those awful stairs twice a day. I almost despised my friend who thought more about her asthma than about things of the spirit. I smiled compassionately.

"Well if I had my way, I would live here."

"Only if you turned into a bat, my child."

We came to the top of the big stairs and entered a small dark room, with circular walls. From the ceiling hung ropes, one, two, three, four in all, one for each bell. On one side Esperança pointed out a narrow weak-looking little stairway that looked like a ship's ladder.

"That's the way you go up to the Holy Mother."

Hanging onto the handrail, I climbed up fearfully and nervously. At the top, in an opening cut in the wall like an archer's loophole, there was a great stone figure of Our Lady extending her arms, and with her back toward me. And because this was the statue of Our Lady of Grace, from her hands hung lightning bolts, formed of strings of electric lights.

I drew near the statue and placed the note in a hole at its base, put there perhaps for that very purpose.

Then I leaned my head forward and looked through the loophole at the street down below, beneath the stone mantle of Our Lady.

At first the view made me dizzy and I pulled my head back, afraid I might faint. Only gradually did I become used to it, and finally, after a series of tries, I managed to look down without fear, saw the streetcars there below, the girls in red skirts leaving the Normal School, the tiny automobiles passing swiftly by. For three months I had not seen the street, people, streetcars, not since the last holidays.

Seen all at once and so suddenly and caught so unawares, the city made my heart skip a beat, moved me so much that my hands began to shake and my eyes filled with tears. Down there was the world, people, the life outside, everything that was forbidden in my sheltered life.

I experienced a violent emotion that combined fear and joy, as when someone steals and takes possession of something longed for and forbidden.

But from down below Esperança called me and I

went down the tiny stairs with shaky legs, drunk with the city, happy to be deluded in my captivity for a moment, with the noise and clash of the living world, of the outside world, resounding in my heart.

And only as I was leaving the chapel, as I was descending the narrow stairway, while Esperança was freeing her skirt, which had gotten caught in the bolt of the door, did it occur to me that I had made no request of Our Lady but had only placed the note at her feet, without a word, overcome by excitement and by the irresistible attraction of "the world."

The exam came and we got the lowest grades in the class.

Maria José never forgave me.

I never talk about my family. The truth is, I hardly remember that I have a family, a father, brothers and sisters, a stepmother.

I have no mother and one who has no mother has no family.

My folks live so far away, lead such a distant and separate life! I hardly feel I know those fat, flabby children, always crying; that nice plump woman, always pregnant or always nursing at the breast, who receives me amiably whenever I come home for the holidays, who has never fussed at me, has always been ceremonious, dutiful, correct, has always given me nice clothes, good shoes, a good school (she deprives her own children to benefit me), so that no one can ever say that she is not good to me because I no longer have a mother.

I call her "Godmother," she gives me her blessing. She herself never wished me to call her "Mother," when Papa spoke about the matter.

"No, no one can take a mother's place." She said, however, that she could be my godmother if I had never been confirmed.

No, I had never been confirmed. Who would have ever thought of that? Perchance my poor Mama, so pretty, so lovely, so ethereal? Would it ever have occurred to her to have me confirmed, if in general she scarcely remembered to feed and bathe me? Poor Mama! So lovely, so childlike, so gay!

I can't say, I never really knew, what she died of; I only know that it was a mysterious brief malady, a sudden pain, fever, vomiting, and death.

I was seven years old when Mama died, and I was away, spending a few days elsewhere. I wonder how that winged spirit of hers behaved in the face of death's mystery? How had her lovely, joyous face looked, always so full of life and light, caught by death's majestic and definitive immobility? I don't know, they never told me. And so I was left with two mental images of her—the first, of Mama alive, the boisterous, childlike young girl who used to take shower baths with me dressed in her short, transparent chemise—

Papa would shout from the porch; he would call Mama silly and shameless, and laugh and say that he was going to come get us, the two of us, with a strap. The water beat on our heads like a scourge, and when Mama would leave the waterspout, taking me with her, we would run through the water-soaked yard, splashing in the tiny muddy streams, the drops of water were cold and hard like little stones and the twigs and pebbles on the ground bruised our bare feet.

The other image—and the one that I could never reconcile with the first—is of my mother dead, the "departed Isabel," as people who knew her say. In the parlor is a portrait of her, in the place of honor, and my stepmother always puts a little blue pottery vase with fresh flowers beneath the picture.

But in her portrait Mama has an indifferent look, her gaze fixed, and her face is ordinary and uninteresting. She looks like a third person; she has nothing of my darling mother as I remember her, nothing of the terrible sadness with which I endow her when I imagine her dead.

When my father remarried, my stepmother gathered in a suitcase all Mama's personal effects, books, and clothing.

I have all those things in my memory; I spent my childhood rummaging through them with curiosity and love, with a consuming jealousy, with an emotion that I am sure will be renewed when I touch them again.

A box of gloves and a wedding bouquet. An empty bottle of perfume, a silver belt buckle, two books: a volume of *The Little Brunette*, and *Les Petites Filles Modèles* by the Countess of Ségur. An album of popular melodies, copied by her in a heavy, round, childish hand.

I suffered many times on account of that handwriting, so different from the idea that I have of Mama, a kind of flighty, frivolous, and smiling angel, made out of all things airy and bright, without weight or form.

The songs are written in a sprawling hand with laborious, bulging capital letters. Poor dear Mama, she must have written so little in her life! Perhaps just in that album of songs and a letter or two to some suitor —No, now I remember something else written by her hand: in the suitcase there is still a prayerbook, a black *Adoremus*, with a cross on the cover.

On the first page Mama wrote: "On the thirteenth of January my daughter Maria Augusta was born. She is chubby and dark and they say she looks like her father which is better than looking like me."

And I don't, Mother dear, I don't look like you. I am melancholy, have gotten large, have neither your laughing eyes, nor your small frail body. On the day of her burial, they said: it looks like an angel's coffin. And it was the coffin of an angel, of an angelic child. Why had she offered a prayer, what unpleasantness had she brought upon her gay self, what sad thought beclouded her heart that day? Those words don't seem to belong to the Mama I knew, but to the dead woman, the other, whom I never saw, and who must have been thinking dark thoughts, still and alone.

My childhood I always divided into two phases: "the time with Mama" and "afterwards."

Much of the time with Mama belongs to legend (and I know that my memories must have many elements of pure imagination): it is beautiful, unreal, like something impossible. And with no continuity, made out of bits of recollections or of things I have heard recounted and imagine I have seen.

They say, for example, that Mama made me go around with a ribbon wrapped about my ears. She was so afraid that her daughter might have floppy ears! I know that I cannot recall this, because I must not have been more than a year or two old at the time. However, the story is so alive to me, has become so much a part of my recollections that I still have the impression of the wide, soft ribbon, encircling my head like a garland.

But there are also real recollections, plenty of authentic ones. I remember Mama on horseback, in a tight-fitting riding coat and black skirt, an enormous skirt that covered the whole saddle. She seemed so very very tall! On the ground, I was crying and holding up my arms to her. And, screaming with alarm, fearful to see me beneath the horse's hoofs, she pulled in the reins and called Papa for help. I wouldn't listen to anyone, had no fear of the heavy hoofs, kept pressing forward toward her. Papa dismounted, grabbed me by the neck, and turned me over to a servant. Then, he got on his horse and led away the horse belonging to Mama, whose image danced before my tearful eyes, who paid no attention to my desperate cries, who ignored my outstretched arms.

I also remember once when Mama whipped me. What had I done wrong that day, telling lies, misbehaving, tormenting an animal? I think I had laid hands on her puppy dog Fantoche, and had started dragging the poor creature by the tail all through the house. It was yelping loudly and scratching the floor with its claws. I admonished it:

"Quiet, Toche, none of your tricks!"

Suddenly I felt a terrible pain, a hand slapping me with fierce blows.

Later, in the living room, while sitting on Papa's lap, I tearfully gave vent to my rage: "She's mean and cruel, and I don't love her any more!"

"Cruel? Who's cruel? Tormenting that poor little dog, about to kill him!"

Mama always argued with me like an equal. Her gentle girlish spirit was so close to my own!

"Afterwards" everything changed at home. Not for the worse, mind you, everyone said for the better. Now there was order, equilibrium, economy. Not so much china was broken, my hair was always combed, and I was clean in my mourning dress. I began to go to school. No longer did anyone see Mama's dresses strewn on top of the bed, no longer did anyone let me play train with the living-room chairs.

Papa got married after five months of being a widower, to a cousin of his whom he had, I think, courted in an earlier day.

His love for Mama had been a sudden infatuation that had taken hold of him entirely, like a spell, sidetracking all things present and past, abolishing all calm and normal plans. Mama had come from somewhere else, had sought the *sertão* because she was thin and anemic, and they had sent her to fatten up, to stay through the rainy season. In two months they had become acquainted and married. Later I was born, she lived her gay birdlike existence for a few years, and when she died Papa resumed his life at the point where he had earlier left off, as if to ask life's forgiveness for that inconsequential, dreamlike, brief hiatus.

Then other children started to be born, fat, listless, well-behaved little fellows. My stepmother also started getting serenely stout, put up the little hammock for her youngest child in the corner of the dining room and spent her time embroidering on the sewing machine great blue and red flowers for furniture covers. At night she made me say my prayers (this was the only time that I ever heard her censure Mama: when she made me make the sign of the cross and I crossed myself the wrong way, inventing my own system, because I didn't even know how to cross myself). She said an Ave Maria for the soul of my mother, who was in Heaven, and I never connected "my mother who was in Heaven" with my dear sweet Mama, so alive, so much of this world, who was always present in my recollections, with her long hair brushing her shoulders, her white dresses with their open lace work, her charming smile, the remembrance of which even today warms my heart.

Everything about my stepmother was formal, proper, and virtuous. It was and is. Because she is solid, indestructible, and unshakeable. For her nothing is banal, nothing is unimportant. She announces that she has a sour stomach in the same grave and sensational way in which she lets us know "that we're going to have another little brother." She beats eggs for a cake with the same austere, concentrated air of someone who is doing her duty, or who is going off to war, for example.

She is good, monotonously good, inexorably good. And, at the same time, an egotist, but with conviction and serenity.

Is it not indeed a virtue to defend one's children, one's husband, one's stepchild, one's dishes? Oh, you should see my stepmother berate the serving maid because she broke a plate! Was it not an attack upon the family patrimony, the destruction of something provided "by the sweat of her husband's brow"?

Heavens, she's not really a wife, she's a Boy Scout.

Papa never listens to her, never argues with her, never expresses preferences or desires. This causes in

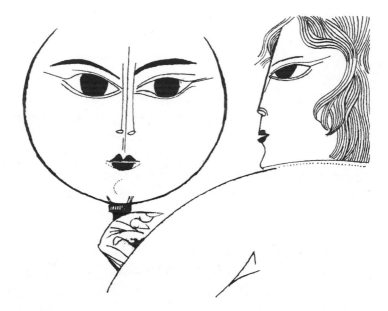

me a kind of sorrowing tenderness, the kind of sympathetic tenderness that people have for one incurably ill who goes to bed and gets up every day under the threat of death.

Papa, however, is healthy and strong, and has only a touch of stomach trouble, and certain bad headaches that affect him after heavy meals. He is fat, sanguine, and serene. Nothing justifies this tender concern that I have for him, and that I suppose was developed in me by the thought of Mama's death. How can he help feeling cheated and cut off from the best and most beautiful and purest side of his life! Having learned to love his first wife with such a great and blinding passion, what all has he not had to suppress in himself in order to be able to adjust to his new measured, regular, immutable life! He, who learned to love and enjoy the subtle charm of life with Mama, who never pointed out her inconsistency, lack of order, childishness. (How he adored her, how he spoiled her! At times Papa would be lying down reading. She would ask to sit down beside him, just on the edge of the hammock, and she would gradually stretch out until she was lying down. She would put her head on his shoulder; Papa would close his book and lie gently contemplating her fine, merry face, so close to his. Then I would seize the opportunity and also jump into the hammock and what fun, what laughter, what hugging among the three of us! Papa always ended up by making both of us leave, looking for his book underneath him, finding it always crumpled, with the pages torn loose.)

Now all this is past history and forgotten. Papa is stern, is a different man, works very hard, looks fat, fat like the whole family. Where are his books? Now he reads only the newspaper.

Where are the poems that you used to teach me at night, out on the porch, with me lying beside you in the rope hammock, we two watching the great red moon as it came up, we two repeating the verses—the verses of the shipwreck—don't you remember, Papa? —about the ship's propeller "which beat like an enormous heart"? The frogs were croaking in the distance, the scent of waterlilies came to us on the fresh night breeze, you stroked my hair, and my tiny heart beat, beat with such emotion, Papa, alongside yours, and I was so happy, so sad, the night was so vast and tender, the verses moved me so, although I didn't understand them fully, that I often kept still and let you go on saying the words, because emotion had closed off my breathing and that enormous, slow-turning ship propeller in the story, I could feel beat—inside me.

For three days now we had been living in a debilitating state of expectation. The violin teacher had asked the Sister Superior to consent to Glória's taking part in his big concert at the end of the year. That annual performance represented the maestro's aim in life, and it was only on account of it that he put up with long months of teaching—compounded of patience and martyrdom—that were harder and more difficult than months of catechism. Only the concert redeemed and repaid him for the obscure cultivation of his flowers. Transitory and ungrateful flowers, like all flowers in this world, which abandoned him in every season. Never in the following year does last year's rising artist reappear; but the teacher accepted this inevitable result of his work as a natural outcome, and he kept on cherishing fresh hopes, like the old courtesan who never despairs of finding her true love, even after thirty years of pretended love.

That summer Glória was the maestro's great hope. She could already play Beethoven and could already make the violin sob in Schubert's "Serenade" as sadly and pathetically as could any romantic gypsy.

And the maestro came to ask this exceptional favor with much ceremony, his white hair more striking and more wavy, his tiny little face more wrinkled and solemn than ever before.

Ma Soeur asked three days in which to decide.

And those three days we spent lying in wait for the Mother Superior in the passageways and furiously discussing the good and the bad signs. Of the three of us, Glória was the most serene, perhaps because her state of exaltation had already reached the point of beatitude. She spent her time humming sonatas, dreaming of applause, laying plans for the Conservatory and for the more distant future in which she would be a soloist at Salzburg and would be playing an authentic Stradivarius, like a Russian violinist who, in a picture she had, was wearing a black velvet dress with a square-cut neckline and train.

Finally the third day arrived, the teacher appeared, Ma Soeur solemnly consented, and that afternoon the maestro's daughter—with a melancholy air and weary gestures—came to get Glória to accompany her to the rehearsals.

We adorned and perfumed her like a bride. And perhaps no bride has ever felt her heart beat faster beneath her nuptial silks.

Glória ended up going every afternoon. And each time she returned it was as if she were bringing us back the whole outside world hidden in her hand.

We would spend the entire day waiting, tirelessly watching the entryway, as if some adventure awaited us too.

Glória came back, her eyes aglow, her face flushed with excitement, and we made her tell us everything (everything!), from the time she had taken the street-car, and a boy in a blue worsted suit had given her his seat; and about the other students who were already waiting in the maestro's rehearsal room; and about what green eyes a young foreign boy had, a fellow violinist, and how he was dark with a sad-looking face.

Maria José, who is realistic and skeptical, made bold to observe:

"He's a coarse Galician. Don't trust him, Glória."

"Don't be so ignorant and prejudiced! He is not a Galician, he's an Arab. I'll bet he's traveled all over the desert, ridden horseback all day long, and slept at night in a tent in the middle of the sands. He might even be a chieftain!"

And Glória also warmed to the subject:

"The world is full of prejudice! What's wrong with being an Arab? Just because he's from a different race, what's the matter with that? And anyhow, he's a Catholic."

Maria José was beaten and gave in:

"If he's a Catholic—"

And from that day on the Syrian lad with green eyes, who sold yard goods over the counter and studied violin in his spare time, came to be for us the supreme hero, the sheik with a glowing white burnoose, who kidnapped maidens from caravans and galloped over the desert with his captive clasped to his heart.

He began paying court to Glória, as soon as he understood the meaning of the looks that she was giving him, and it was as if he were courting all of us, because all three of us began to love him, although Maria José and I had never seen him. Glória, however, related and described so much that it was as if he lived unmistakably and eternally among us. We knew what his hands were like, long, dark, and with a diamond in an ancient setting on his left ring finger. And when his wrist vibrated in playing a tremolo, the ceiling light also reflected on his diamond ring, and we could see, rising from his hand, a light that was as brilliant and tremulous as the voice of the violin. He wore light-colored silk shirts and gay ties with a wide knot. He had black hair, wavy black hair that at times fell down in his eyes; and then with his hands pressing upon the instrument, he would shake his head backward in a bold romantic gesture. He used a subtle and delicate perfume, and Glória, on her return, would give us her hand to smell—the hand that he had held—so that we too could smell his perfume. And we would steep ourselves in those details that Glória repeated interminably like a marvelous tale, our hearts opening wide to her confidences and enjoying also their share of love.

He could speak French, had been reared in Europe —or in Lebanon—and used to converse with Glória about Pierre Loti, who began to be for us a kind of god.

One day, finally the concert took place. It was Glória who presented the professor with a great bouquet of luxuriant roses; the maestro gravely kissed her hands, as if in tribute—and there the dream ended. Or rather, the dream entered upon a new life in our memory, since it could no longer be nourished by that wealth of de-lectable detail brought every day by Glória.

The sheik—this is what we used to call him—had spoken of love on that final day; he had made veiled allusions to the future, to the sweetness of a life together lulled by their two violins. And when they said good-bye, he made a promise that Glória communicated to us with feverish apprehension, as if she were plotting a crime.

And, in the evening when it was almost dark, we went and sat down in the Normal School patio, the only place in the Colégio separated by only one wall from the street, which was furthermore a poor dismal-looking side street, sloping and tree-lined, where no one ever walked except an occasional tardy churchgoer mincing along, saying her rosary.

We waited a long time, fearful and weak with anxie-ty, our pulses beating hard. Suddenly, in the calm of the patio, someone on the street could be heard whistling the first measures of "Rêve d'amour." Yes it was, it was our sheik! The beloved melody scaled the wall and came to us with a flutelike trill, sharp, mysterious, and en-chanting. He was fulfilling his promise, this sheik, and he came to serenade his sweetheart with the music they had played together. We couldn't answer, nor did it occur to us. We stood pressed to the wall, listening with all our strength: every measure was like an inspiring and unforgettable word, was like the very voice of love calling to us and spiriting us away, carrying us to the vast airy reaches of the world, where the passions dwell —the world of unreal happiness which allowed us, poor cloistered children, a tiny glimpse of its magic brilliance.

My heart beat, beat with love for that man, whom I had never seen, whom I was never to see, as it has perhaps never beat so strongly for any other. My emotion was so intense that I feared Glória's jealousy. She, however, had no such thought and was happy to feel that her love was shared by us, and perhaps she felt the need to divide with us that weight, so great and so sweet, that filled her heart.

We continued staying close to the wall, silent and oppressed. The music began to fade away gently, and a sharp pain went through us when the marvelous sound completely stopped. We could now hear his footsteps on the sidewalk, slow, hesitant, then deliberate, rhythmical, as they drew away.

When the last sound had disappeared, Glória turned to me and whispered:

"I could at least have said: *Merci!* No one was listening but him!"

And she laid her head in my arms and cried.

My distress was as great as hers, so great that I turned my head away for fear that Maria José might see that I too was crying.

We were just beginning dinner, at three o'clock. Aurinívea, "Granny"—the reader for the day—was preparing to begin the meditation, and had already said the sacramental phrase in her thin rasping grandmotherly voice:

"In the name of Our Lord Jesus Christ! God's holy name be praised!"

And the hungry lot of us had shouted "Amen!"

We were in the act of cutting our meat, with knives that were eternally and incredibly dull, when Sister Germana entered, flushed and flustered, whispered in French to the Sister of the refectory, and both went walking around between the tables examining the girls' faces, one by one.

I heard Sister Germana say as she passed near me:

"Ce monsieur a tout vu, ma soeur, la voiture et le jeune homme—" How pale they now were, the two of them, and how upset!

After their anguished search, they hardly noticed us, nor did they even see our anxious eyes. Finally, they left together. And as soon as they passed the door, there ran through the entire refectory, from ear to ear, a mumbling from the tables of the older girls:

"Some girl ran away. Isabel heard Sister Germana say so."

Who had run away? And with whom? And why? No one knew.

Also disturbed, we looked around at each other, trying to see which one of us was absent.

Sister Germana and Sister Vicência came back, carrying the big roll book, which had everyone's name. The roll call began:

"Hortênsia! Present. Enedina! Present. Maria do Carmo Silva! Present. Present—Present—"

No one was eating, dinner lay forgotten on the plates, and it was the Sisters, always so careful of discipline, who were causing the disorder.

"Maria Estela Pontes!"

"Absent!"

Someone spoke up:

"She went to the infirmary."

The procession continued:

"Maria Augusta—Josefina—Alba—Angélica—Luísa Lima—Luísa Correia. Present—Present."

"Teresa Pinheiro!"

No one answered. Sister Germana repeated:

"Teresa Pinheiro! Where is Teresa?"

No one knew, not even Celeste, her young sister.

"Didn't she go to the dentist?"

The little girl, now trembling, got up from her place.

"No ma'am, yesterday was her day."

The roll call continued but no one else was absent except Teresa. The Sister singled out two of the big girls, spoke to them in a low voice, and they left, very gravely. Afterward she ordered us to finish dinner in silence. But silence was impossible. A suppressed murmur ran from place to place, and with it the story which some of the girls had gathered from the Sisters' conversation:

"A girl has run away! Teresa. Her sweetheart was

a resident student at the Colégio Cearense. But how and where did she get out?"

Suddenly everything stopped still, and you could hear an excited voice in the corridor outside, and Sister Germana ran to the door.

And the Mother Superior appeared, pale, her lip quivering, holding one hand tightly against the other on her bosom, as if to hold back her tumultuous gestures. Nothing could be heard now in the big dining room, not even the sound of tableware. No one ate any longer, no one ventured a word, and we were all shaking with tremendous fright, as if each one of us had also run away and was now awaiting punishment.

The Mother Superior stood looking at us for a while trying visibly to calm herself. I, who was nearby, heard her reply to a question fearfully whispered by Sister Germana:

"Bêtes, je n'ai vu de cas pareil que chez les bêtes aux champs!"

Slowly, still containing herself, she thrust her slender white hands inside the sleeves of her habit; finally she spoke:

"My dear children, I have come to seek solace with you. This house has been covered with shame, one of you has run away from the school, run away to the arms of a man. Worldly love has driven her out of her mind, sin has blinded her, she has become like an animal of the fields which knows no shame, nor fear of God, and heeds only the diabolical counsel of her instinct. She has forgotten the parents who love her, she did not care to consider the scandal to which your innocence would be exposed, she has not thought of her own immortal soul which has been placed in peril! My motherly heart has been terribly wounded and I come to weep among you."

However, the tears she had in her eyes were not a mother's tears. Her speech lacked sweetness, her pathetic words did not move us, but rather inspired fear as if they were laden with threats.

Unlimited authority seems to cut Mothers Superior off from all source of humble and loving emotion. An outraged queen, she suffered much more for her dishonored house than for her lost child. That was, at least, the feeling we got from her words and from her agitation.

The Mother Superior turned toward Our Lady, guardian of the refectory, a beautiful china figure found in all the dependencies of the Colégio. She looked at her for a while in silence as if asking the holy woman for serenity and counsel. Then she suddenly knelt down, folded her hands, and intoned our ejaculation: "O María, conceived without sin—" and we gave the response, uneasy and confused.

But we did not finish the prayer, as we were interrupted by a loud convulsive weeping, and screams, and the noise of something falling. Celeste, Teresa's little sister, was having an attack. Sister Germana, kneeling on the floor, took the girl in her arms and gently shook her, exclaiming: "Oh my child, my little child! Jesus! Maria!"

The girl was screaming and writhing, as if her despair and shame had been transformed into a devil who was possessing her. Tears flowed from Sister Germana's eyes, ran down her cheeks, and in her alarm she could only go on repeating:

"Lord Jesus! Poor little thing, poor little thing!"

Now she was different and truly wept. She really did feel like a mother, and she cried.

Teresa had run away with her sweetheart, a young fellow no less youthful than she, who was also forced to reside at school by his family.

Eternal Romeo, eternal Juliet, once more these two lovers had been born and taken shape, had both started life upon the same green slopes of the Serra Grande; in the same school they had learned their ABC's, but shortly thereafter were separated and turned against each other, each taking his part in the ancient hatred that for years and years had been envenoming their people. Later, as adolescents, they started to fall in love, without anyone's knowing how it all happened, after so much bloodshed, so much crime, so many curses. Spied upon by everyone in that small territory, they could scarcely manage to see and speak to each other. They made up for it in letters, written at night and read at night, fearlessly exchanged at the greatest peril.

One day the boy's father, powerful in the *sertão*, intercepted one of the letters from Teresa. He sent it back to the chief of the other clan, the girl's father, with a sneering note, implying the worst insults.

Teresa got a beating with a braided whip and the next day she was taking ship at Camocim, headed for Fortaleza, where internment in school, a kind of criminal exile, awaited her. And the young man, who had run away after her, beside himself with longing and with rage, was apprehended here also and forced into a school run by monks.

At the Colégio, no one was well acquainted with this taciturn, friendless girl, who was always daydreaming, perhaps mulling over her rancor and her plans. Only one sentiment did she manifest, and only it gave humaneness and warmth of life to her enigmatic figure: this was her love for her sister, a little twelve-year-old girl who had come to the school a few months after her, since her family now wished to head off at an early stage any new romances. Teresa looked after Celeste like her own child, and never did the rigors of discipline prevent her from putting the girl to bed, from tucking her pillow under her head, from kissing her the first thing in the morning on getting up, and from putting her shoes on for her. Only once did she raise her voice at the school: to protest about the little girl's food, a tough, gristly piece of meat. On a certain occasion, also, she found an older girl laying hands on Celeste. She beat the other girl so violently that only the collective efforts of a Sister and ten or twelve of the girls managed to pry her hands from the poor girl, whose uniform was ripped to shreds and whose nose was bloodied.

On account of that Teresa was almost expelled. Isolated in a study room, she was punished for several days by being made to copy on an interminable number of pages this single sentence:

"Je suis une bête féroce."

A thousand times she wrote it, perhaps more. Her punishment, however, did not soften her, and it even seems that the force of repetition had an effect on her and that she was more silent, unapproachable, and fierce than ever.

"Bête féroce" were the words of her punishment. "Comme une bête aux champs," the Mother Superior used to say. And actually, what else was Teresa, if not a handsome young animal, vigorous and rebellious, capable of every audacity in order to break her shackles, to pursue her destiny, and to go after her mate along the vast high roads of liberty?

Gradually the details of the escape came to light.

Teresa had gotten money together by patiently saving the small quantities which she was given for lunch and pin money. She had communicated with the boy, they had planned their simultaneous escape, and she had sent him her savings.

On the appointed day, at precisely three o'clock, when the dinner bell was ringing and the whole school was on its way to the refectory, an automobile was waiting for her near the chapel fence, with the boy inside and the motor running. Since noon Teresa had been wearing street clothes underneath her blue uniform. She went through the chapel, took off her uniform, and left it on the doorway steps, where it was later found. Calmly she climbed the outside fence. On top, she hesitated a moment, sensing that the hem of her skirt was caught on one of the spikes of the iron grating. But her indecision lasted only a moment because she resolutely hurled herself forward, thereby tearing her dress, and fell down on her knees near the car. The boy inside tried to come out to help her, but she immediately got up; only the young man's hand was seen helping her in, then slamming the door of the automobile, which disappeared around the corner of the alley.

A tavern keeper on the opposite side of the street witnessed everything and did not even have time to shout and call people, so fast did she climb, leap, and make her getaway. The man went yelling into the entry hall and related the events so poorly that the little old woman at the door did not understand him and thought he was crazy or drunk.

Celeste had become ill with shock and had not yet stopped crying on the day following the escape, when the person responsible for her came to get her. And what hurt her the most, her sole complaint, was that her sister had not said good-bye to her.

After three days, the Colégio was still under a pall as if in mourning. Never in its fifty years of history had such disgrace been brought upon it. We didn't dare speak above a whisper, even out of earshot; no one sang, and we were forbidden to allude to the incident.

Our thoughts, however, never left the runaway, but followed her automobile through the long streets, and dwelled upon what she must have been feeling during the mystery of her nights, along the roads, or upon her awakening to adventure in strange places.

At night Maria José, Glória, and I, seated on the grass in the patio, lost ourselves in these imaginings. We would stretch out flat on our backs, our hands under our heads, gazing at the Three Marias which shone nearby and called to us. All around us the walls rose up higher now by more than half a meter to prevent new escapes. Here and there scattered bricks, heaps of mortar, the disorder of construction. But, what did we care about walls, the highest and most secure prison? We had our stars.

We had our stars and several other problems. The problem of Jandira, for example. A case of a bad beginning and an obscure outcome. Jandira was an illegitimate child; what's worse, the child of an adultery. Her father was a married man and her mother a humble, mix-blood prostitute. Jandira didn't have any definite home, she lived with her aunts, her father's sisters—three old maids, only one of whom esteemed her—and she did not know what kind of future lay ahead of her.

People think that children are unaware of life's dramas. And they forget that these dramas do not obey discretion or choose a proper moment; naked and fearsome, they reveal themselves indifferently to the eyes of adults and to the eyes of children. For example, Jandira's history, unsuitable for minors, raised terrible questions for us and attracted and disturbed us unceasingly.

Jandira hated her other two aunts. She felt they treated her like a miserable, importuning animal, like a bedraggled cat which has been let in during a thunderstorm at night, and which has a right only to the crumbs of charity—to its saucer of milk on the floor and to a humble spot on the hearth, without ever being permitted to curl up on the living-room pillows.

And Jandira was ambitious, precocious, imaginative. She wanted a place at life's feast, and not the least,

nor the most obscure. And she used to fight for it. She
slept late, polished her nails, turned up her nose at certain dishes on the table. She stood at the window, watching the young military cadet who was strutting with
the air of an aristocrat and showing off his golden epau-
lets. She would smile at him and later boast of receiving his military salute and of the number of times she
made him turn back down the street.

Dondom, her youngest aunt, who was myopic and
ill-humored, used to observe:

"Know your place, my child." And it was as if she
had struck her in the face.

Jandira would come to the Colégio, throw herself
into our arms, purple with desperation: "I'd rather she
had given me a beating! I'd rather she had killed me!"

And nothing moved them, these diabolical old wom-
en, not the achievements which the girl threw in their
faces, nor her honorable mention at school, her success
in public speaking, her pride, her invincible ambition.

"Know your place, my child—" (That is: "Think
about who you are, about the mother who had you, a
woman without a husband and beyond the law, who
abandoned you to be brought up by charity. Ahead of
you life looks beautiful, attractive, glittering. But for
you it's only a showcase: don't stick out your hand;
you'll hit the glass; and don't break the glass; you'll
come out bleeding— Be satisfied to look, and, if you like,
you may even desire. But stop at that. Go to the Colégio:
study with the others, wear what they wear, laugh with
them, play with them. In matters of the heart, be like
them, and, if you like, learn what love is, read books
about it and dream! But when your time comes, stand
back, don't have anything to do with the sentimental
lad who will come to serenade you, don't dare think

about a boy of good family, but look for someone of
your own kind. Never forget, because no one will ever
let you forget, your original stigma, the blemished
womb that formed you, and the day that ever saw you
born had best be put out of mind.")

Injustice was a familiar thing to us, and in general
we did not go into the reason for things. To us, orphans
were orphans; sick people were sick people; poor people
were poor people. But injustice, in Jandira's case, was
all too close and evident. It hurt us all.

In Maria José's opinion, Jandira should have gone
and become a nun: "Since the world doesn't want her,
let her seek out the arms of Our Lord."

And I would comment, with bitter irritation: "A
nun? What order would take her in? Do you think that
there is room for her in any convent? Only as a lay
sister, in certain orders, or as a penitent, in the Order
of the Good Shepherd—"

As if Jandira would ever agree to being a lay sister
or a penitent! Mother Superior, abbess, prioress, nothing less.

Jandira was an extern. She saw much more of the
world than we—the avenues, the movie houses, the
young men—and she felt its attraction at closer range.
And at times she went through strange phases. She
forgot all about the question of "her place," calmly occupied the place she wished, and fraternized with her
tyrants. She chose friends from the aristocratic circles
of the Colégio, fell in love with the brothers of these
girls, deluded herself, laid plans, courted the enemy,
and perhaps even made over him a bit.

We felt we had been betrayed and anxiously awaited
the inevitable comedown. And the comedown came,
as suddenly and brutally as a slap on the face. Some-

one had said to her, in one way or another, somewhere on the most unexpected occasion, the same old line:

"Who do you think you are? Know your place."

And we took her in, sympathized with her, planned vengeance. We dreamed up impossible marriages, as in books. It is true that in books one always finds out that the little schoolmistress with no one in the world is of noble origin, the daughter of a count and countess. And with Jandira inescapable reality was always there, present, scoffing: her mother still living, taking lovers, degrading herself, bearing more children, as invincible and unconscious as a force of nature.

And I would murmur, looking up at the dark sky, my hands joined behind my neck, thinking of something that, in last analysis, might perhaps be a solution: "I am afraid that she is going to finally kill herself."

I was about to reach my fourteenth birthday when, for the first time, I had a desire to kill myself.

Naturally I had no reason. I believe that what we customarily call "motive" is in such cases of secondary importance: that is, some concrete, immediate cause which is responsible for the suicidal impulse. Those who need such a motive kill themselves by accident. But the person who wants to kill himself does not need a great and irremediably tragic pretext; he kills himself indeed by reason of that obscure aspiration of his to die; he kills himself because something within him calls, because he feels a violent and invincible attraction.

It is like love. Why does a woman passionately desire a particular man, why does her flesh quiver at his touch, at the barest brush of his hands, at the simple suggestion of a caress? Perhaps love for death is like love for a man, and she is satisfied, is consoled, and is cured only after being possessed and exhausted.

I know that since that time I have always considered myself to have suicidal tendencies. I was afraid, afraid of the act, afraid of the pain (now I am back to my analogy), and my fear was mingled with desire.

And I consoled myself a little, for my dissatisfaction, by talking and thinking about it, by planning gentle and obscure deaths—sleeping pills in the silent hours of the night, or a dash into the sea from the solitude of a deserted beach.

And when I spoke in confidence about this, no one believed me. Maria José and Glória called me crazy, Jandira mentioned the holy Scripture: "that a suicide is the same as a murderer."

They would laugh, make up verses about me, ridicule me; and if they talked about me, it is because that age loves discussions and takes pleasure in controversy.

And they doubted me to such an extent, they so summarily ruled out my fantasies, after proving their logical impossibility, that I myself was at times convinced that my morbid desires were a farce, that I was engaged in play-acting.

Meanwhile, my secret aspiration remained, and has always remained. Today I have it more than ever.

Sleepless nights, long interminable nights; my eyes dried up, my body tossing in bed without finding a soft place to rest, my hands digging soft holes in the pillow, weariness, such a weariness! The sluggishness of the dawning day, of eternal, immutable things which are going to be implacably repeated. And dreams, dreams of an impossible blissfulness, of a sweet and rapid death without pain and without misery, a death as joyful and cunning as a dream, precisely like the dream that I never have.

Before the holidays of the final year, Jandira surprised us with sensational news: she was engaged to be married. For some months she had acted aloof: we thought that her studies were occupying her, whereas she was concentrating on her plans, preparing all alone her escape, fearful perhaps that we might put objections and difficulties in her way and take away her courage.

Her fiancé was a seaman, slow of speech and deep-voiced, lumbering in his gait, a simple soul; he gave no heed to the tragic origin of his bride-to-be; he wanted only a wife and he wanted Jandira.

His romantic calling compensated for their inequality, and eliminated certain distances. A seaman is unconsciously a kind of poet and the sea is the ideal backdrop for all lyrical tales. He had a gasoline launch and transported cargo from the ships to shore. Jandira didn't tell us if she loved him and perhaps didn't even think of that. It was enough that he loved her. (Strange and marvelous thing for her—she who was always supposed to "know her place"—to feel that she was first in the mind and heart of another.)

And she showed us the gifts from the man she was to marry, the cuttings of silk, the bottles of perfume, the heavy wedding ring, her wrist watch. However, she never showed us his letters, those he wrote on a trip he made to Camocim. She told us merely that they were terribly passionate and lovesick, and so bold that if Dondom had seen them she perhaps would have called off the wedding, scandalized and enraged.

One day I saw his handwriting in a book he had given her. Irregular, awkward, childlike. And from his handwriting I imagined his letters. That is why Jandira never showed them to us.

Jandira married on the day she became eighteen.

The altar was decorated with roses and lilies, and the bride wore on her breast the blue ribbon of the Daughters of Maria, along with her white silks and veil.

I never understood why—whether out of spite for her aunts, vengeance, mockery, or simple human kindness—Jandira had her mother attend the ceremony, her ignored and unacknowledged mother, the cause of all her humiliations. She discovered her, I don't know where, dressed her up, showed her off, and fell into her arms after the wedding. And her mother did not disappoint her: simple, modest, wearing a plain, dark coat, she gave her blessing discreetly to her daughter, smiled tenderly, and disappeared.

Her aunts wept, especially the eldest, who thought well of Jandira, who used to hold her in her lap when she was little, and tell her stories; we knew that when the girl got engaged her aunt gave her for her trousseau her own "hope chest" of lace—lovely, tenuous lace yellowed by the years in the shadows of the drawer, collected for her own wedding, which had never come, faded and ancient like dried flowers.

Jandira embraced the old woman, hung on her neck, and wept as one forsaken, wept as I had wept the day I entered the school. Our eyes were also filled with tears, and the bridegroom, touched and bewildered, timidly smiled and seemed to be asking forgiveness for being the cause of it all.

Finally a car drew up to the sidewalk, and Jandira got in it with her new husband and her mother-in-law.

At night, lying in our dormitory beds, we would think about her, who was our age, and who was already wearing a gold wedding band on her finger, already walking on the arm of a companion along new and free roads.

The atmosphere there oppressed us, and it seemed to us that they were imposing excessive years of childhood upon us. We felt a humiliating sensation of failure, delay, lost youth.

No longer a child, but still not a mature woman, I was taken from the warm and cozy retreat of the Colégio—and I finally came to know the world.

After the holidays that followed upon our diplomas, I found myself at last in the city—settled—on my own.

I was supposed to have stayed at Crato; the holidays weren't supposed to be holidays, merely the beginning of my new life at home with my family. I, however, did not go along with that, and I spent those months at home as in a hotel, as in a way station. It embarrassed me to say so, but I did not consider that to be my proper home, or what's worse, I felt no need of a home, and everything seemed to me boring, monotonous, and inappropriate.

At school, in all our compositions and in all the songs at year's end, one sang about the beauties and the delights of home. For that reason, perhaps, my deception was so great.

The youngsters bothered me, I had no love for them, I felt toward them merely that conventional tenderness that I had been taught in books, "the loving-kindness one should show to his younger brothers and sisters." I found them hostile, spiteful, obstinate. They broke in on my moments of meditation with their arguments and crying spells, they constantly fought, yelled, soiled themselves, and were malicious, thoughtless, and cruel.

It was only with the passing of time that my love for children became developed. On that occasion, I was seeing my brothers and sisters too close up, children I was not acquainted with, who merely wearied and frightened me.

Later on, I always had that same fear and that same uncomfortable vague fatigue whenever I found myself in the disturbing and incalculable proximity of a crowd.

When I first got back from school, I would with great enthusiasm run to them with open arms. I expected that they would ask me to tell them stories, that they would sit on my lap, sweet smelling and angelic. But the youngsters were continually dirty, wanted nothing to do with me, and, in the midst of fights and confusion, never got interested in stories except very vaguely. And if I attempted to be helpful they would poke their hands in my face.

At home the monotony was so oppressive, so constant,

that it came to be as painful as a bruise. I started turning black and blue with boredom.

On the very next day after my arrival a solemn session was held, in which, after a brief prologue, Godmother explained my new duties as a daughter and older sister, and spoke of the help that the family expected from me. And, oh, how horrified I was, Our Lady of mine, at the beds to be made, the stockings to be darned, the tables to be set and cleared, those never-to-be-forgotten weeks that I was supposed to alternate in the kitchen with my stepmother! The much-lauded aim of all that was to prepare me to be the future mother of a family, the wifely producer of a brood. I, meanwhile, merely felt that they wished to take advantage of my presence in the house, to get work out of me, and this of the most uninteresting and inglorious sort.

And no one understood me, and they wondered why, after so many years of cloistered discipline, I should only wish, only aspire to, freedom and prohibited pleasures. As if the prisoner ever got used to prison, and as if he, after being freed, should desire nothing more than to return to his prison uniform and his evening rounds in the patio!

My dream was to sleep late, without screaming children, without the sound of the broom throughout the house, without that laborious and exasperating movement of a beehive at dawn. Without the voice of Godmother, who would open the door to my room, clap her hands, and say sonorously:

"Maria Augusta, look what time it is! You know your father doesn't like for you to sleep so late! We're already having our coffee."

I, who would still be taking my ease, thinking vaguely about things pleasant and indefinite, would leap from my bed in fury and embarrassment, slip on my dress in all haste, go and wash my teeth at the window of the dining room; there I would forget myself once more and daydream, my mouth full of foam, looking out at the beds of zinnias.

Implacably, with the shrillness of something mechanical, Godmother's voice would be raised anew:

"Did you make your bed, Daughter?"

All my blood would rush to my face, I would rinse my teeth in haste, run to my bedroom, and pull the blanket over the wrinkled sheet. I still heard Godmother's comment of veiled censure, to Papa:

"After so many years of school! How is it possible that she never got the habit?"

But, Lord in Heaven, she couldn't see, Papa couldn't see, no one could see, that the sole desire in my heart was to uproot my habits, forget about the slavery of the school bell, prayers, made-up beds. Why get out of school, why be a woman after all, if life was going to be the same and if growing up had not delivered me from childhood?

It is hard for me to express in a few lines everything that that decisive period meant to me, which would perhaps require a book, and nothing less, to speak of my rebellions, my nighttime tears, my desperate wish to run away, which got to be almost an obsession.

The best thing to do is to move along.

So then when I saw in the newspaper the public announcement of a competitive examination for a typist's job in Fortaleza, I clung to that hope with such tenacity and energy that Godmother gave in, Papa gave in, and he brought me to take the examination, saw some friends of his, and got me the job.

I began work. And it seemed to me that my happiness was about to begin. To live by myself, to live for myself, to live on my own, to be free of my family, to be free of my roots, to be alone, to be free!

And in the city, life was equally monotonous, full of other little tedious duties. Everything ran along in a routine which I steadfastly wished to believe temporary, but which became implacably fixed.

I was eighteen when I started to work, and six months later I had already started to fear getting old without ever knowing what the world was all about.

The world—my thirst for it was great. Not for pleasures, or rather, not solely for pleasures. My soul was like that of the soldier in the folktale of Pedro Malasarte who abandons everything, sets out with his knapsack on his shoulder, experiences hunger and persecutions, walks covered with dust and weariness through strange cities governed by cruel and crafty kings, all plotting his downfall. He, however, a slave to his desire to "see," to "know," confronts all things, continues eternally in search of the impossible surprise, of things never seen, journeying always ahead, beneath the sun and through peril.

I felt I was like him, that the two of us were brother and sister, the soldier and I, and I was his sister who stayed behind, who could not accompany him, and who held out her arms to him and wept.

To be on the move. To live. To live a complex life, where people really exist, love, suffer, die, and do not know what it is to spend their lives sitting at a machine typing cards and more cards, turning out reports that others have written, vile and inhuman things, words which have no real existence and no contents, which designate nothing except the absurd relations of persons who are themselves only a formula or a title. Words like "Your Excellency," for example. Phrases like "health and brotherhood."

First I went to live in a pension in the home of one of Papa's female relatives. But the room was dark, small, and costly; all the salary from my job went for expenses there, and I never would have worn a new dress, never would have had a change of shoes if I hadn't from time to time received some gift from my stepmother—always something solid, good, horrendous.

Afterward, I went to live with Maria José. Dona Júlia had given up the dairy, which brought in nothing but losses and struggle. She had moved to the end of the Mororó line, near the cemetery, was selling box lunches to support her children, and was always tired and nervous, complaining of life and of people, eternally alert against the evil tricks of destiny. A clairvoyant of bad luck, she foresaw its blows just so she could suffer them in advance, and every sorrow that others counted as only one came to her twice: before and afterwards.

Maria José taught at a school in the outskirts. She shared her room with me. Large and bright, with windows opening on the street, it was in the front of the house, where the living room ought to have been.

Each one of us arranged our possessions round about the bed, and the only piece we had in common was an immense old wardrobe, which had come from the Alagadiço house. Dona Júlia also kept in it her good clothing, which was no longer the old straw-silk dress of former times, but rather a new one of light checkered silk that rustled. And two little sailor suits belonging to her sons, red flannel trousers and blue blouses, which had belonged to the older boys and now served for the two younger ones. Dona Júlia could never open the wardrobe and look at the sailor suits without sticking out her lower lip and shoving the hanger farther into the corner, with an unvarying, angry gesture. It had been the last present from their father, her husband whom the current had carried away and who today was sailing through distant and sinful waters.

Beside her bed Maria José had a kneeling desk and, on top of a corner shelf, figures of Christ and of Our Lady in plaster of Paris; on one side, a little table full of school books and notebooks to be corrected, her veil, her thick prayer book that she took to mass. Above the corner shelf a charcoal drawing that she had done at school.

I had obtained a little shelf for my novels and poets, mingled with a few loose numbers of the *Official Journal*, which the office obliged us to subscribe to and which only Dona Júlia read, "to see the list of new appointments."

At the head of my bed was a portrait of Papa and

Mama, a stiff discolored photograph, in which Papa looked more faded and seemed to have more of a phantom air than his dead wife.

Reading in bed, on Saturday afternoons, we would many times stick our heads out the window as a rich funeral procession passed by (why are there more burials and weddings on Saturday afternoons?).

The great hearse covered with gold leaf, the four rigid purple bouquets shaking at each corner, the red-and-green mound of funeral wreaths crushing the deceased, the long slow-moving line of automobiles, where now and then a young man would turn around to look at us.

Maria José would cross herself and whisper some sudden ejaculation on behalf of the soul of him who was returning to "the great country." I would take the opportunity to make some ironic remark in bad taste about the other world, some disparaging allusion to the decomposition of the poor soul who was passing by on his bier.

Because I must say that a good while ago I had broken away from the religion I had brought from grammar school. The process was slow, like a gradual dissolving, with neither surprise nor violence. The truth is that I never really believed in anything; faith was, for me, an exterior shell, and my greatest act of faith was perhaps to become lyrically excited by the mysteries of communion and of ecstasy, to assume a prayerful attitude, "to feel" the devout person within me, as the actor on the stage feels within himself the personage whom he incarnates.

My failure to practice it gradually showed me the weakness of my faith. I ceased believing because I ceased praying; I ceased immediately to feel my "personage" within me when I no longer played it as a role. I gradually abandoned religious practice—evening prayers, mass, confession—and my convictions were lost. I tried to hang on to them, and perhaps it pained me a bit to get off the beaten path that others walked, to lose that mystical support, which to many people is like a moral crutch. But I didn't struggle hard, or I didn't struggle at all; I let my belief go out of my heart like some water trickling through my fingers.

It is true that, for my very own benefit, I stirred up fictitious controversies which, in final analysis, bored me. I didn't have to enter into discussions to lose my belief; I had nothing left to destroy; why then go on fighting? However, I let myself be drawn into debates with the Sisters, with Papa, with the Rector—perhaps through a certain love for oratory and polemic, and through the very adolescent desire to scandalize, to set myself apart, though condemned for it. I wrote letters, I appeared at interviews where we were to discuss the doctrine of evolution, original sin, and the cause of the angels' rebellion. I read thick books of exegesis, partly to satisfy Sister Germana, who hoped to win me over with the word of the church doctors, partly to obtain arguments with which to make up for my ignorance. Strange and obscure books, often full of a primitive, subterranean poetry. One of them, *The Divine Mystique*, described the witches' sabbaths, the diabolical masses, the apparitions of the devil, a great black animal seated on a throne of flames, adored by souls that had fallen victim to pride, ambition, and lust.

The book was beautiful and terrifying, and at the same time ingenuous and majestic. I have never forgotten it.

I did not last long in the polemic; the role was fatiguing for, after all, the whole affair did not interest me; it was like digging up withered roots.

I felt no profound need to talk about those matters, except for that occult desire to mystify in order to make myself feel important. When I wrote the final letter and appeared at the final interview, it had already been such a long time since I had stopped thinking about God! And, as I look back over it, since my childhood, religion has perhaps never been for me anything but one of my school subjects—one of those which has pleased me most, rich in profound suggestions and in invincible poetry, from the shepherds of the Bible to the trumpets of the Final Judgment.

Was it about this time that Glória became engaged? I think it was. She told me of her plans in a brief lyrical letter, very different from what one might expect from Glória's energetic and almost harsh temperament. She spoke of her "dear fiancé," a college graduate from the interior (from Quixeramobim, where the Mother Superior had sent her to spend the holidays), a well-liked and amiable young man. I was envious. In my own future, I did not see any intelligent and marriageable young college men. Nor doctors, nor soldiers, nor naval officers. I was flirtatious, but shy, and did not know how to coordinate my suitors. I dissipated my efforts in streetcar flirtations, simple glances, smiles, furtive words. Glória's engagement excited me more than I cared to admit. At the Colégio we had gotten used to experiencing the other girls' love affairs as romances common to all.

I met Glória's college man when she came back from the holidays. He was timid, delicate, and well read. He talked about good authors, although without warmth, a fact that made no great impression on me, because at that time I continued not to read anything that could really be called a book.

The young man called Maria José and me "Glória's little sisters," and brought us boxes of candy as he did for his fiancée.

Now that she was happy, Glória reigned magnificently, and her role was always the foremost, as in the dark days of her tragedy. She lived her hour of love with the same tireless and passionate fervor with which she had lived her drama; and it seemed that her lover had entirely taken over the place earlier occupied by her father's tomb.

Maria José, who had always considered Glória's filial devotion as a superior virtue, came and asked me one day if I too did not think that Glória's unbridled love for her fiancé was not a kind of betrayal of the earlier limitless ardor of her longing for her dead father. And that shook me. I too could now see the betrayal; it grieved me that Glória should thus renounce him after so many years of filial widowhood.

And we were both mistaken. Glória's heart had not changed, it was ever the same, despotic, generous, passionate.

She needed to love ardently, and for years she had clung to the shadow of a dead man. Then a living person had emerged, had insinuated himself in her tenderness, had made himself loved, and—nothing could be more natural—all the force of Glória's love became channeled in his direction.

And I envied her. It is true that it was not exactly because of her young college man, who, as a person, did not interest me much. Only once, when I came upon them kissing, did they upset me a bit. What I envied was the opportunity to love, was that tranquil right to possession of a man, of a living person, that Glória arrogated to herself, and his happy submission, the joy he seemed to feel in quietly holding her hand, the smile of tender acquiescence with which he allowed Glória to introduce him: "Afonso, my fiancé—"

I began to have soaring dreams. I wanted to fall in love with an exceptional man, different from all the rest—a blind man, for example. To be the light of his dead eyes, the only link between my beloved and the world, to surpass through an uncommon love the unexciting and routinely happy love affairs that humiliated me.

Was this perhaps the influence of those war novels, full of mutilated heroes, which were our reading material in those days?

But I reached a point where I could not imagine myself loving a man except as his nurse, embracing him and shielding him at the same time, giving myself entirely to pay for his lost sight, arm, or leg. My still imprecise maternal instinct seemed to need to find somehow or other something weak to protect.

Afonso had taken us, Glória and me, to the theater. I put on a brand new dress and new hat, and I felt that I was older, prettier, and different.

The curtain was lowered and raised again, the entire audience was still atremble with the vibrations from the piercing high C.

Downstage, the tenor bowed in gratitude, his tiny eyes gleaming in the brilliance of the glaring lights. I applauded with enthusiasm, and I felt my heart now gently warmed with the exciting music; at my side, excited too, Glória and her fiancé, their fingers intertwined, the languorous and dewy eyes of each fixed upon the other, smiled nervously. I felt touched and alone, seeing their love so close to me and still feeling the effect of the idyllic scene and of the amorous and melancholy manner of Don José.

The tenor withdrew, the curtain fell for the last time, and I looked about at the people around me, at the quick-breathing multitude in the orchestra seats, who were now releasing their emotion in violent hand clapping.

It was then that I noticed the man with greying hair, sitting in one of the seats reserved for the press. Lean, without color in his face, his features small and fine, with bushy hair streaked with white, which flared around his palid temples. He was homely, weak, small, but he had a romantic air, perhaps even an air of inner grandeur that he sought to project entirely through his enormous, deep-set, dark eyes. He looked at me at length, fixedly. And I looked at him, at first unconsciously—the man was so old!—afterward half disturbed, still under the influence of the lovely melodies and of the physical charm of the tenor, sensing unconsciously in the man a false and theatrical air that was quite proper to him there, which made him seem to be a part of that entire fiction of painted backdrops and false faces of which we in the audience had seen so many.

The man, seeing my eyes upon him, lightly smiled, and made a slight gesture of salutation to which I responded, without really knowing whether I knew him; of course I did. How else would he dare to greet me if he had never seen me before? Moments later he stood up; he walked smoothly, deliberately, a bit stooped. He leaned against the railing, and stood smoking a long, thin cigarette, exhaling the smoke with a meticulous pleasure, letting the two columns rise from his nose, slowly, ritually, like incense.

And he did not stop looking at me, with such an insistence that it would have been indiscreet had his eyes not been beclouded with smoke, becoming distant and seemingly dim.

I turned away, anxious and somewhat distressed. Glória, in complete ecstasy, smiled at me through the veil of love which was also blurring her sight. I felt more lonely than ever, and suddenly I was grateful to that man, to that gaze which sought me out in the midst of my desolation.

In the half light of the large room, his figure stood out delicately curved, like that of a little old man, and he seemed to me still more romantic, thus silhouetted in the shadows. Afterward, Carmen began to sing, Don José once more made love to her; I plunged anew into the opera. Only once did I look away, letting my eyes rove among the figures closest to me. And I noted, with a jolt, that, half-reclining in his seat, his attention far from the scene, the man was still watching me in his indolent way, as if only the sight of me compensated for so much tedium.

With him began my first love affair. It should be noted, however, that I truly deserved compassion. I was still not twenty, and I felt completely alone; my hopes in the world and in its promises were at a complete crisis.

I saw him the next day. His name is Raul. We were passing in front of a café, and there he was at a table, all alone midst clouds of cigarette smoke.

By day he seemed older to me, more tired. And also more romantic and mysterious, with a promise of great moments.

Maria José, who was accompanying me, saw him when he spoke to me. She too knew him. He was a painter and led a wild sort of life. It was even said he took cocaine. A drifting, shiftless Bohemian who was acquainted with half of Europe and with all the cafés of Paris that were the haunts of artists. He had almost died in a hospital in Naples, from which he had managed to be repatriated with a falsified emigrant's passport. In one of the vicissitudes of his flight, he had arrived here years ago, and, no one knows why, had married here, afterward taking his wife with him from luxury apartment to luxury apartment in good times, and from one third-class pension to another when things got bad. Emerging from a new crisis, he had now come back, seeking his father-in-law's hospitality in order to rest a bit. He started painting and selling his pictures; he found pupils, and for over a year now had stayed around. He used to come home in the early morning hours, his wife would make trouble, and the whole neighborhood heard it all. He was worthless.

I heard his biography without surprise; it was the only story that would tally with him and with what I had imagined about him.

The café was on the corner and Maria José and I took the cross street, rounding the corner. I saw him once more, he straightened up a little, and his deep-set eyes smiled at me, emerging from their fog. I smiled too, attracted by the terrible promise of his history of vice and adventure.

In my sleep that night I thought of Raul. I saw his pale face very close to mine, his look that spoke of grief, his mouth with its trace of bitterness. I discovered a strange beauty in that face.

A few days after the theater and the café a young fellow, a mutual friend, whom I knew on the street-cars and avenues, introduced us. He was one of Raul's acquaintances from the park benches in the Praça do Ferreira, where they furiously discussed art and politics.

It was at a band concert, and they were playing "The Blue Danube." We talked of Strauss waltzes and Vienna. As if making a discovery, Raul told me he thought me intelligent, spoke about his painting, promised to show me some of his pictures, and invited us to go to his studio.

I was afraid to go, but I went. I went with Aluísio, the same lad who had introduced us, and with Maria

José: I enticed her with the prospect of seeing pictures, real pictures actually painted by an artist, and not prints; and with the prospect of seeing Raul in the act of painting—an exciting experience for Maria José, who gave painters and musicians her wholehearted devotion and to a certain extent included them in her court of saints.

And Raul in no way disappointed us; he turned out to be exactly the kind of artist we had dreamed of, dressed in a white smock, lost in the enormous room with its clutter of easels, drawing boards, and pictures.

In one corner of the room, in a black frame, a picture done in Paris. The Seine, the docks, the dark mass of houses beyond, fading into the mist. And in addition other pictures from Europe, landscapes with poplars, a golden evening in autumn, two nudes. One of the nudes was of an old woman with her back to the viewer, reclining on red velvet cushions. It caused me sorrow and pain. Raul, however, stopped behind me and said with conviction: "This one is good." Perhaps it was good. But to me it only hurt and embarrassed me. How could it be good, that poor old undressed grandmother, so ridiculous and unhappy?

Everywhere nudes and more nudes. Maria José, whose curiosity was pure, could adapt herself to so much undraped pink flesh without fear or embarrassment. Was not art something sacred? Was not the Vatican full of nude statues? And she expressed her opinions and asked questions. I was much more uneasy, and it seemed to me that somehow Raul intended to drag me to see his collection and put me in the midst of all these women who were exhibiting on canvas their breasts, their bellies, their thighs. And I was thinking about

precisely that, as Maria José and Aluísio were commenting on the Seine landscape, when Raul approached me,
touched my arm, and said,

"I think you would make a nice portrait, you know?"

I recoiled in consternation. Me? Not me! I immediately saw myself, also naked, on the divan, posing like
the others.

I turned toward him abruptly:

"Me? Never!"

Raul was insistent: Why not? If I could but see myself at that moment as he was seeing me, my gaze pensive and dark, my profile set off against the red background of the wall—

"I'm dying to paint your hands and your eyes."

Maria José came up and asked if he had ever devoted
himself to religious painting.

Yes, once he had done a Christ that had not turned
out well, an Annunciation that had been left at school,
two or three saints that others had commissioned.

"And I was just this moment seeing if I could get
Guta to pose as Our Lady."

"Our Lady?"

I smiled. Maria José, however, applauded enthusias-
tically. "Yes, Our Lady— Our Lady was a Jewess and
must have been dark-skinned too."

Raul looked at me, his eyes closed, and smiled. "Our
Lady as an adolescent, with her arms full of flowers—"

Aluísio, who had finally left the Seine, listened to the
rest of the conversation and protested:

"There's no resemblance between Guta and Our
Lady! You're talking a lot of nonsense! Do a modern
painting, old fellow. Guta at work!"

"Right, as a typist, which I actually am. That's the
only thing I look like."

Raul and Maria José found themselves in noisy agreement. He, who would have agreed with anything, and who naturally had never thought seriously of painting a saint, was just then sketching out the picture:

"You stand there, Guta, behind that table. That's right, with your white blouse fastened at the collar, your typewriter beside you, with a faraway look in your eye, and your stenographic notebook forgotten in your hand—"

"I don't know stenography!"

"You will in the picture. And the picture will be called 'The Secretary.' That's the way I always imagine you, at your office."

I protested. I spent my days at the office with my fingers dirty from carbon paper, hunched over my machine, typing one report after another—

Maria José, who was not listening to me (she hated to see me use the common elements in life "to create something spiritual"), was already arranging with Raul the details of my posing. I could easily come in the afternoons, after four. From four to five, for example. Whenever she could get away from school she would come with me. And she concluded innocently:

"I don't think there's anything wrong with her coming alone. You, sir, are no longer a young fellow, which might cause people to talk—"

I looked toward him. Raul smiled inscrutably, agreeing:

"Oh, yes, I'm an old man, already out of date—"

I kept trying to find a way to keep from coming, but I couldn't think of anything. Raul was now explaining to Maria José and to Aluísio the terrible difficulty he found in working in a country without models, without anyone able to sit, either professionally or as a favor.

Little wonder that he shouldn't now want to take this unexpected opportunity of counting on Guta, who represented such a different type, with such unusual eyes and smile—

When we went downstairs, Raul accompanied us as far as the door, and as we went out he held on to my hand:

"See you soon, Miss Secretary. May I count on your bringing her Saturday?"

Maria José loudly swore she would. Aluísio also promised to come back soon and return the books he was taking.

It was I who said not a word, and I left almost in fear; in fear that, though I had actually said nothing, I had promised more than the others.

And he smiled from the doorway, likewise promising, and of course expecting God only knows what.

When Aluísio left us, I advanced upon Maria José with my teeth clenched. Had she herself not told me about Raul's unexemplary life, his drunken sprees, his eternal carousing? How could she compromise me with that business of the picture and posing?

Maria José, meanwhile, beguiled by what she had seen, and perhaps too innocent to have noticed anything, didn't pay much attention to my recriminations:

"Now, Guta! He limits his running around to 'a certain kind of woman.' Who would ever think of talking about you? And besides, he seemed to me so cultured, so educated, so artistic! There must have been a lot of malicious gossip."

And she didn't perceive that the danger lay precisely there, in his being "cultured," "educated," "artistic." I felt like telling all I knew and throwing cold water on her enthusiasm. But I refrained and thought reasonably: "Tell what?"

On the appointed Saturday I went for the first sitting. I was accompanied by Maria José and Aluísio, who were very much interested in the portrait.

It was a holy day and no street noises rose up to the *atelier*, just the incessant song of the Cathedral bells. Raul got ready for me to pose and spent a while thoughtfully studying my face, in profile, full and three-quarter views.

Maria José, amazed and full of respect, so excited in the presence of this sacred rite she could hardly breathe, had sat down on one end of the divan and remained as quiet as could be, her hands on her knees, her gaze rapt, her mouth agape.

Aluísio, as usual, was leafing through the books he kept finding on various tables and was paying no attention to anyone.

I was the one who didn't much believe in the seriousness of these goings on and in the earnestness with which Raul would take my chin and turn my face slowly to find the best light. I saw all this as a farce and as a pretext hiding dark designs. It's true that the idea of the portrait, of the painting, of his choosing me as a model, a choice that was almost a gesture of love— all this turned my head and dazzled me. I spent two

nearly sleepless nights, thinking about the portrait, creating the picture in my imagination, recognizing myself on the canvas, seeing my hands, my eyes done in that dull light,.with that motionless, distant, mysterious look of figures painted in a studio.

But that was beforehand. Now, however, alongside Raul, I felt him all too near, a proximity that took away much of the "artist's" magic essence. He would smile and talk, sketching with brisk strokes on the big canvas, only the back of which I could see on the easel. And his eyes kept going over me insistently, as if undressing me or touching me. Then came a moment in which he said:

"Keep very still and I'll draw your mouth."

His manner of speaking sounded to me as aggressive and blunt as a stolen kiss, as an act of possession. My lips were trembling and I could feel upon them the weight of his bold hand, which was now deliberately, amorously, at work sketching, as if it were softly touching my mouth and slowly taking possession of it.

The other two saw nothing and sensed nothing. Just he and I. I couldn't bear it for long and had to interrupt him with the pretext:

"May I see?"

Raul put his hand up toward me precipitously:

"Don't come now! It isn't worth seeing, it's still a rough sketch!"

I, meanwhile, was already beside him and looking with admiration, and some disappointment, at the angular figure, with all my features accentuated, which he had sketched in imprecise lines with charcoal.

Raul was insistent:

"Your mouth is extraordinarily hard to master."

He smiled and added:

"Will it always be so hard?"

I went back to my chair. Aluísio, who was now sitting down, quietly smoking, was looking at me fixedly, as if he too were studying my face. Half smiling, he too was minutely observing me, but I sensed nothing, nor saw in him the sort of eyes the other had.

Maria José had stepped behind Raul and was accompanying his hand movements, the twitch of his mouth, the way he held his breath. He sketched for a while longer, removing, renewing, rather nervously. Finally he burst out:

"Let's stop. Guta must be tired and I can't do anything more."

Maria José sighed with regret.. The painter covered the canvas with cardboard and allowed no further looking or commenting.

"Let's let the sketch rest."

And he went to show us an album of English paintings, which he had spoken about a few days earlier.

I, however, left them looking at the album and went to steal a glimpse of the canvas. Truly, it must be me. Ugly, a complex of rigid lines—that's the way he saw me. It was painful and humiliating to find this out. If he saw me like that, then it was impossible that he should ever love me, that he should ever desire me and idealize me. And they say that he who loves what is ugly, finds it pretty—No, this is not true. And the proof is that I was seen by him, who seemed to love me, as even more ugly and misshapen, as though in caricature.

I was thinking about all this when I became aware of Raul behind me. He had left Maria José and Aluísio busy with the album and had come to whisper into my hair:

"Now, when you leave here, I shall no longer feel so alone."

Taken aback, I ventured:

"I'm so different there—I hardly recognize myself."

Raul laughed:

"What about your inner self?"

Frivolously, I looked at the sketch, its nice resemblance. But the expression, the inner feeling, is what interested him: "And I believe I have caught precisely that. I even managed to register the best of your expressions, that half smile of yours with your lips curving downward."

I kept still, flattered to see him so interested in the finer points of my expression. But deep inside me I really didn't believe it and started thinking that perhaps he wasn't after all the great painter that people around here thought he was, underprivileged people who have never seen anything and can have no opinion about artists.

Or, to put it another way, art was really just one more deception.

Glória wanted to tell Jandira about her marriage and we both went to visit her, where she now lived, on a street over toward Piedade. It was a big old house; vast rooms with stuccoed ceilings, an enormous, dark ground floor, porches with wrought-iron railings, and dilapidated windows. A palacelike structure abandoned by its owners, a rich man's long-forgotten caprice, the ancient, solitary house jutted above the small hip roofs of the humble dwellings along the poor street.

I found Jandira thin, wearing very modest-looking clothes, her hands rough and her nails chewed, and with her eternal air of defiance, which meant that she was suffering.

We had heard that her husband had started drinking and now spent his time loafing and didn't come home to sleep.

We tried, discreetly, to learn the truth. However, Jandira said not a word, didn't complain, and referred to her husband in a friendly fashion. Who knows whether she hated to trouble Glória's hopes with her own disillusionment, or whether she kept silent out of simple pride, which is more likely.

She showed us her child, who was now over a year old, was afflicted with an eye ailment, and could hardly see a thing. He stayed in his little hammock, quietly sucking his rubber pacifier, counting with one hand the fingers of the other. Apparently his mother spends the day with him, sewing. She seems to support the family with what she earns at her machine. She at least told us they were having a hard time: her husband had lost his boat, was out of work, and she had to help a bit— and as she spoke she was finishing a piece of sewing, rapidly, as would one who knows what time costs.

We left there sad, full of bitterness. Glória said no more about Afonso or about the furniture she was picking out. And I could not forget the little blind boy, so still, already at that age knowing how to be resigned, receiving misfortune like one who is to blame for it and who accepts his punishment.

When we got home I gave a big hug to little Luciano, Maria José's youngest brother, who was waiting for me at the door.

He is a quiet child, as soft as a cat, and he has big green eyes that are sad and curious, that overflow with tears at the slightest provocation as if, so green and so limpid, they really were made of water. His eyes can see, they are alive.

Overjoyed to see him, I sat down and took the little fellow in my lap, ridding myself of the feeling of gloom, of repressed anguish, that the blind child had given me. Luciano was startled by my embraces and the pensive way I looked at him:

"Holy gee, you act like you're crazy, Aunty!"

He was a dreamer, liked to lie in my lap, and stay there, silently thinking, biting his nails, which perhaps helped his meditation. He called me "Aunty" and said he loved me more than his mother or his sister. He had a horror of going to school, was scared of the teacher, hated his lessons and his homework. Kindergarten romps never appealed to him. To him it was all school, a taboo word so terrible and abhorrent that he never uttered it. Whenever he wished to refer to his school, and he referred to it as little as possible, he said uncomfortably: "There."

I always slept late in the mornings, as the office wasn't open until eleven. Almost every day at a definite time Luciano burst into my room and hung on to me, screaming; Dona Júlia chased him with soap dish and towel in hand. That bath of his, followed by school— poor Luciano considered the life he led and his whole family to be unfriendly, heartless institutions.

"You dirty, obstinate little pig, you!"

Luciano held on to my shoulder, not saying a word and clenching his teeth.

"Let me, Dona Júlia, let me take him—"

"You know, Guta, I'm going to wear this kid out!"

And Luciano, once more in tears, would be dragged out by the ear, fussing at me because I turned him over to his mother.

Then he found himself a dog. It was a yellow and white one with a thin curly tail, a street dog, a boy's dog, a happy friendly cur. For two days Luciano whined around after everybody looking for a name for this mutt. His big brother proposed "Lion," "Fido," "Rex"; and Maria José, "Jaloux," "Kiss," "Flirt"; and Dona Júlia, "Medoro," "Shark," "Sawfish"; but Luciano, hard to please, kept shaking his head. A stupid name. Terrible. It sounded like the name of some dog in a book (he hated books). I suggested: "General." Luciano smiled and was happy. General!

And General chose me to look after him. The two of them hung around me all the time when I was reading. Luciano with his head in my lap, thinking his idle thoughts; General, lying on the floor, now resting his muzzle at my feet, now snapping his teeth in the air at passing flies. Later, as if by agreement, the two of them would arise with a bound and rush out laughing like a pair of souls possessed, turning over chairs and making the floor shake.

There were days when Luciano didn't know his lesson at all, had to stay in at school, and caught it when he reached home. He came weeping to me. He muttered words of abuse against his mother. He said he was going to live with his father. As if his father wanted him, silly boy! His father had another child, a little boy who went around in a red velvet suit and a lace collar.

Another day we were walking down the street, Maria José and I, when we met the little boy and his mother. Maria José's hands turned icy cold, she grabbed my arm, and it was all she could do to say:

"That's the woman, Guta—"

The woman went by, and if she recognized Maria José, she didn't show it; she bent down and took the child by the hand and went into a store. After they were gone, I observed:

"So that's his—his child?"

"Yes—that's my brother."

What must have been Maria José's feelings, leaving out shame, of course, upon meeting this brother?

The same feelings I have in the presence of my godmother's children? I really don't have any particular feeling, and there she was crying. And, like my brothers and sisters, that child also belonged to another woman. And, at least, her own mother was not dead. She lived in her own house and was not buried in the ground. There was no plump, orderly stranger of a woman sleeping in her bed, putting flowers around her picture. Maria José, at least, could see her own sweet mother at any time, and kiss her and listen to her complaints and console her. There are people who are worse off. In the meantime, it was she, not I, who was crying. Everyone thinks he has a better right to cry than I do.

Jandira's little blind boy doesn't cry either. Her little blind boy with veiled eyes, so alone, so resigned!

I put Luciano down from my lap. It was better for me not to look at him too much then.

Maria José came in from work, tossed her purse on the bed, and came over to me:

"Know something, Guta: today I met Aurinívea, 'Granny.' She's going to be a Sister, naturally. She's awfully thin and laughed when I called her 'Granny.' —And she talked about the girls and even told me one horrible thing. You remember Violeta? Violeta, the one in our second class, remember? Well, she's a prostitute."

Of course I remembered Violeta. She used to run around with us now and then, although she didn't belong to any group. She was a rebel, an independent spirit, and never was close to anyone.

It's true that her physical make-up did not fit the hardness of her spirit. She was large and very fair, with a softness about her big eyes and a nice gentle smile, when she smiled.

At heart she was tender and sensitive. She liked animals and children and was the one who took the best care of her plot in the class garden. And all she planted in it were green vegetables which she wouldn't let anyone pull and which matured and withered there, useless.

"At least give them to the poor!" the Sister told her.

Violeta looked boldly at the nun:

"I've never seen any poor folks here."

She was by nature indolent, fond of eating, and pleasant; but deep within her she had unsuspected reserves of rebelliousness and was capable of terrible rudeness; with a frightening thoughtlessness, she could come out of her laziness and calm and haughtily get even when she thought she had been offended, making a Sister blush and tremble with humiliation and rage. And at times it was not out of vengeance but just out of a hostile instinct to fight, "a sudden attack of meanness," as she would say afterwards. Her principal weapon was passive resistance. Only rarely did she resort to sterner measures: "when I have to impose my will—"

In general, it would happen like this:

"Violeta, answer the second question!"

Violeta would look at the Sister out of her big gentle eyes and say nothing.

"Answer, girl! At least say you don't know! But say something!"

Violeta would keep looking at the Sister and say nothing, with the same ingenuous air of challenge. The question might be repeated ten, fifteen, a thousand times, and she would remain impassive, outwardly unmoved. At times the Sister would desist and take another topic and another student. Or she would get mad and take the matter to the Mother Superior, before whom Violeta continued to wear the same silent smile, the same disdain. She could hold out indefinitely like that. Or suddenly break her long silence with some harsh, unkind, and unexpected word that was like a slap in the face.

I don't know why they didn't expel her. But I heard a lot of talk about exorcism, and I believe they would have exorcized her if they had not feared some unforeseen trick, perpetrated in the priest's presence by the demon who inhabited the girl.

And a lot of people at the Colégio believed in such a demon. We knew plenty of stories about people possessed and about the saintly Gema Galgani, the flower of purity and piety, to whom the devil appeared daily in the form of a lion, a serpent, or an octopus, embracing her, crushing her, devouring her. And the miracles of Lourdes, where young girls possessed by Satan fall on the ground screaming before being sprinkled with drops of water from the fountain. Then there was the story of the girl who went to the dance and, as her dress had a low neckline, tied her miraculous medal around her leg. There a handsome young man appeared and danced with all the girls but her, and she wept with envy. Later they found out that the youth was the devil. She had been saved from dancing with him by the miraculous medal, even tied around her leg.

And in addition there were all the possessed in the New Testament and in the lives of the saints.

Violeta herself seemed to be proud of her legend and liked to show off her demon.

It's true that I once saw her crying. It was at evening recreation, and we were all alone at the far end of the covered veranda. She dried her eyes when she saw that I was observing her; her lovely blushing face became redder still, and her eyes grew brighter. She laughed in my direction, with no good reason, or with some imaginary reason. She started talking about herself, her mother, with whom she didn't get along, her little brothers and sisters, whom she adored, the old Negress at home, her confidante, her friend, her mentor. When she talked about her mother, you could see quite clearly a cruel misunderstanding between the two of them, the mother trying to dominate her daughter in hopes of educating her, the girl retaliating with the Negress's arguments, and, being supported by the Negress, reasoning fiercely and primitively just like the Negress. In general she called her mother nothing but "she." Rarely if ever did she use the affectionate term "Mama." And she talked on and on, telling of her troubles, her revolts, why she was so rebellious, why she didn't study:

"I don't study because I don't like to and I'm lazy. And even if I did like to, I wouldn't study, so as not to give 'her' that pleasure. Matilde [the old Negress] always tells me: 'Study, girl, study! You're white, aren't you? White folk's lot is to learn!' But I don't want to learn, I want to be like a Negro. When I don't have any more Colégio, I'm going to work in the kitchen. In that house I'll stay only as long as it's in the kitchen. Just think how satisfied 'she' would be if I walked into the living room and played the piano, or embroidered fine table linens!

"To tell the truth, Guta, I would really like silk dresses, hats, and jewels. But 'she' takes the joy out of everything for me. One day I lost a ring, another time I tore a new dress. And she came and scolded [and she imitated her mother's ugly, metallic voice]: 'So you lost your ring, eh? All right then, give me your bracelet, and you can only wear it when you get some sense in your head.' 'So you tore your dress, did you? Well you won't get another one 'til the end of the year.' I screamed that she could keep it all, and never buy me anything else, that I didn't care. Today, she begs me to wear a gold chain or to put on a little crepe dress. I won't wear jewelry, I won't put on a dress, and I go around at home in my old school uniforms; and when I put on my good uniform for going out, I make sure I get it dirty right away, and tear it right away, so

I won't give 'her' the pleasure of seeing me as well dressed as the rest of the girls—"

And now Violeta had become a streetwalker, a prostitute. I interrogated Maria José in every way possible, to learn the details. She, however, knew almost nothing and had scarcely asked any questions of "Granny," horrified by her words: "She's hopelessly lost—"

I kept thinking about Violeta's beautiful eyes, her shy and gentle spirit. And now she was living by her body, and her door was open to all men. And I tried to imagine the horrors of such a life: along comes a fat man, with a big hairy moustache, smelling of beer, and he has the right to come in and lie down in bed with her and make her do whatever he wants. And I could almost see the man, his shirt smelling of sweat, his fat lips drooling, his flabby flesh. Or then some other sort—thin, scrawny, old—with adhesive plaster crosses on his neck, or smelling of cigarette butts. And others, Lord God, any and all. Now I looked with new eyes upon all the men I met in the street, that I saw around me, on the streetcar; I saw them in a way in which I had never imagined them; I placed them inside a woman's bedroom and they made my flesh crawl with horror.

In my memory I could see Violeta's arms, round, white, her bosom, which she always bound so tightly, covered up so carefully, being more modest than the other girls. And now—

Suddenly, I thought of myself. Wasn't I also on the road to perdition, falling in love with a married man?

But I couldn't make myself believe in that idea. Raul represented to me, at that moment, love, and as such it was pure and intangible, above all things and all people, above good and evil. And if I frequently felt remorse, if at times a submerged good judgment made me realize the shamefulness and immorality of that love affair: he, a married man, I, hardly more than a girl (If Papa knew, if the Sisters at the Colégio should guess! What secret pleasure they would have in saying: "She has no religion, she has no faith, she was bound to go astray!"), I would put such thoughts aside and forget them, deep in ecstasy.

"A married man." In truth, perhaps, the romantic, the unusual, the forbidden aspects of this adventure were what most attracted me. To think that I should be capable of such a great love that I could overlook the risks and the prejudices. He, an artist, "misunderstood," married to a stupid woman, came to seek support and comfort in my heart. By what right could I deny him that? Why be ashamed? Instead I gloried and was proud.

Of the tremendous power of intimacy and of the common bed I had not the least idea, nor of anything else. I imagined that he was tied to his wife merely for the sake of convention. Raul only alluded to his wife as to some distant, different person, almost an enemy.

And I supposed that she meant nothing more to him, and I perhaps thought, very secretly to myself, that my expression of a desire would be sufficient to make him sacrifice her at my feet. For that reason, I took pleasure in sparing her. I only wanted to some day bring about an explanation between the two of us—an explanation in which I would defend myself against her accusations (which were, of course, the accusations that I kept making against myself), in which I would explain to her the nature of our love, and the rights which such a love gave me, and, particularly, the right of Raul to choose freely the course his heart should follow—

And my love drew its entire sustenance from such fantasies and absurd dreams. That was my way of loving, and to be sure, it was not precisely Raul that I loved—almost an old man, not handsome, and with no other attractions for me except his beautiful language. his paintbrushes, the halo of art that he wore and that transfigured him in my eyes. If he had been an ordinary sort of man, a bachelor, a suitor, I would not have had eyes for him.

At that moment, however, I was not concerned with that sort of speculation. I was concerned only with loving him, with loving him in my fashion, more and more intensely, and with imagining impossible trips, unthinkable adventures.

The portrait was coming along.

We were in the fifth or sixth sitting, and I had gone alone to the *atelier*. Raul was expecting me and had put the chair in place and was already sketching on the canvas, "composing details," as he put it. He received me without putting down his palette, had me take off my hat, and started immediately to work, laying in large strokes of ochre on what was supposed to be my face, where already a pair of immense, dark, morbid eyes stood out.

It was plain that he enjoyed painting, and it even seemed that this was one of his ways of taking women for himself: to paint them. Or perhaps he was recreating on canvas some other young woman, who was at the same time a fabricated and a living thing, his own handiwork, and a strange and desirable object, the possession of which afforded him an anticipation of the caresses and pleasures of the real one.

After a quiet ten minutes he stopped painting, started soaking his brushes in a glass of turpentine, and smiled:

"Now we're going to sit down over there and chat a little. I admit that I'm tired."

I let him sit down beside me, take my hands in his, and tell me all those sweet words of love that we dream of all our lives, even after we're disillusioned old women. But it was obvious that his heart wasn't in it, that the words were hard for him, that he was somehow in a hurry or secretly disturbed and was thinking of something other than what he was saying.

Finally he quit talking altogether, looked down at my hands, and began to twist Mama's ring, a little pearl in a gold band, that I always wore on my left hand.

"Guta, I like your hands. They're slender and delicate and warm—I like your arms—"

And he let his lips pass over my fingers, my wrist, lifting my sleeve in order to kiss higher up, as far as my shoulder. Now he was pressing his face to mine, and I could smell close to me the perfume that came from his thin, gray hair, and I could see the wrinkles around his eyelids, his tragic mouth with its heavy lips and the burning, pleading, unmistakable gleam in his eyes.

When he kissed me—this was the first time anyone had ever touched my lips—I felt a shock, almost repugnance. It was moist, tepid, and strangely tasteless —but I let him. My heart was beating fast, in fear and complicity. It didn't last long, however. He himself withdrew, startled by I don't know what. He sat looking at me for a while, distantly, as when I was posing. Then he turned to my arms and began to kiss them again; he wanted to paint them, now, showing them just as he saw them in the sunlight that was coming through the windowpane—round, soft, golden.

And I took a deep breath, feeling much calmer, and I let him nibble my fingers, cover the palms of my hands with kisses.

Someone knocked at the door. He jumped from the divan, so brusquely that I was frightened. He ordered me to resume my pose, took up his brush, and waited for another knock to come.

It was a friend of his, Ramos the poet, who was out looking for a bit of art.

He saw us doing the pose, and hid his little perverse smile, but I clearly saw the wrinkles of suspicion around his eyes. I was now composed, however, and managed to speak pleasantly with the man, trying to cover up the mute ill-humor displayed by Raul, who had hardly looked up at the poet. Ramos flung himself down on the divan, stretched out his long legs, and fumbled in his empty pockets in search of a cigarette. He did not know me, but it was apparent that he was interested in knowing who I was, scenting a romance, of course. He waited a bit, could contain himself no longer, and exclaimed to Raul:

"Hey, Rembrandt, you're so absorbed in your art that you're forgetting the simplest conventions! Why don't you introduce me to the young lady?"

I looked so innocent with my straight hair and white blouse, my pencil and notebook in hand, that I had no fear of his getting any wrong ideas about me. I smiled good-naturedly at Raul, who quickly looked at me out of the corner of his eye, as if consulting me:

"The poet, Belarmino Ramos—you probably already know him, Guta—And you, my friend, are looking at Miss Maria Augusta, who is being good enough to let me do her portrait."

I had already heard of the poet and had recognized him as soon as he came in; I said so. And he was flattered and said complimentary things—quite clearly I was a lovely and intelligent young lady; the very fact of my sacrificing hour after hour for art, modeling for an ill-tempered painter—

Finally Raul was willing to set up the unfinished painting and let it be subjected to the learned commentaries of the poet, who suggested modifications. He went to a cabinet and came back with a bottle and glasses. He poured me two fingers of kümmel. It was sweet but burned like fire. I coughed, the poet was amused, and Raul watched us with somber superiority, sipping his liqueur in his unfailingly grand and stage-struck manner; then someone opened the door below; there was the sound of footsteps on the stairs, and his wife walked in.

If I had drawn a picture to fit my preconceived idea of her, Raul's "legitimate" wife, it wouldn't have been far from the truth. She was the classic wife, the bossy kind, mistress of her house and of her man, just as she is imagined in jokes and by women who think all men misunderstood and who like to seduce other women's husbands.

She was almost pretty, but stout, with a thick waist and common-looking hands. She was well dressed, but there was some indefinable something of poor taste about her, perhaps a lack of confidence in her choice of clothes, a characteristic of women who don't go out much; her travels and adventurous life with her husband had been of no help to her. She gave me a hard look, one of instinctive mistrust, it seemed to me. Fortunately I was near the poet, sitting modestly on the edge of the divan, with my glass in hand. Raul didn't introduce us, nor did it occur to him. He merely said to her:

"What are you doing here?"

And I could tell that she was his wife from the very unmistakable way he spoke, that was part intimacy and part tedium. And from the very way in which he laid his hand on her arm a few moments later. It was not a caress, my feeling told me, but as if he were putting his hand upon the easel, the curving edge of the divan, or any familiar piece of furniture.

Though understanding the whole thing, I felt jealousy. He, of course, had no idea that I could feel anything. But his wife was so commanding, so sure of herself and of her rights, looking at me silently from beneath her little yellow straw beret, as if waiting for me to ask her forgiveness and go away. Raul called her over

to see the painting. One could see now that he was trying to put us at ease, and that he wanted to make her
like me.

She however did not care to cooperate, looked at the
picture without interest, and said laconically that she
did not see much likeness. Then she called to him and
led him over to the window; they stood there whispering
about money matters because he took out his billfold
and withdrew a banknote. And I felt terrible and more
and more like an intruder there, vaguely fearful of the
other woman's unyielding antipathy, hating her and
imagining impossible little scenes—for example, like
Raul's offering me his arm and our walking out together, leaving her there by herself; or his taking my
hand again, as he had a few minutes earlier, and kissing
it right before her eyes.

I observed Raul. What had become of his earlier
look, his trembling lips, his dark pleading eyes, his
restless feverish hands? Now he was another person,
sure of himself, completely changed. He resumed talking with me, half-heartedly, trying to be witty; he
roused the poet, who immediately came to life, and
launched noisily into a tiresome discussion about sur-
realism.

The lady, lukewarm, sat there keeping an eye on
things. Now I envied her her smooth white skin. I have
never had great ambitions, except in moments of gen-
erosity and fantasy; but I am full of small vanities.
and the charms that this woman had and that were re-
vealed to me little by little—charms I lacked—humiliated me intensely. I kept thinking of the comparisons
that Raul would of course make between us, and I continued studying her with envy and regret.

I discovered she had big feet that looked ungainly in high heels, and I looked happily at my own, fitted in a schoolgirlish little pair of slippers.

I felt I should remain silent and didn't concern myself with the conversation, sensing that this was not necessary to my role; it was better for me to continue being retiring, discreet, and to limit myself to the simple role of model. And I was completely engrossed in these comparisons when the poet, the climax of the discussion having passed, turned to me:

"Shall we be on our way, Dona Guta?"

His tone suggested complicity, and his invitation as well. He was taking advantage of the momentary confusion, breaking in upon our duet, and acquiring rights. For the first time that afternoon Raul gave him a friendly look, and I suddenly hated both of them, hated her, hated myself. But I could see by my wrist watch what time it was, accepted, and told Raul that I might not be able to sit the next day. Maria José had not come to join me as she had promised, and tomorrow again she might fail me. He bowed politely. I don't know if the lady understood my excuse. Belarmino, however, intervened once more:

"Why not count on me? I'm always here at the sittings. I can also bring you!"

(How could he stand there and lie in my name, in our name? And I was going to accept, I had to accept!)

I politely said my good-byes, left husband and wife on the landing, admitted the poet's complicity, let him hold my arm to help me down the stairs.

And I was able to get rid of him only much, much later, after we had gone to the city square, and after we had had a vile dish of ice cream together that was gritty and sour.

Finally I caught the cemetery streetcar, in which there was an entire family in mourning, carrying enormous sprays of cheap flowers, poppies, marigolds, and zinnias, all in red, yellow, and purple.

I spoke of people going to the cemetery. I too used to like to go there, in the afternoons, to get Maria José, who would be coming from the novena in the All Souls' Chapel. Sometimes Aluísio went with me and seemed to experience a particular delight in those walks we took among crosses and weeping willows, gravely chatting about transcendental matters, about the soul and life, heaven and earth, God and nothingness.

He was timid but at times would unexpectedly come out of himself and confide in me at length: talking about his father, a backlands judge; his mother, eternally sick—consumptive, worn out with childbearing, praying and waiting for death; his soldier uncle in whose house he lived, a loud, patriotic despot; his high-school days, banal and sporadic, his school chums, his few real friendships. He had never had a girl friend. He never talked about girls and seemed to be living in some kind of expectation; perhaps he believed in a great love which would come into his life like an irresistible summons that would be his redemption.

"Redemption from what, Aluísio?"

"From banality, from mediocrity, from everything mean that humiliates a person—"

He liked to drink—he even came around to admitting it—and I knew that he had affairs with women; that is, he made a habit of going to those second-class pensions where young men and prostitutes apparently sometimes form almost familylike associations. In moments of confidence such as those in the cemetery, he himself used to tell me the things he heard from them, the familiar, pathetic story of the woman who had a daughter with the nuns in a convent school and who at the end of the month would fight with the other women over their customers, importuning acquaintances to scrape together the money for the monthly room and board, unexpected expenses for a new uniform, books for French class and chemistry. Or about the other woman, wretched thing, who was on her deathbed in the Charity Hospital after taking permanganate in a jealous fit over a chauffeur; or about the little sixteen-year-old who had been knifed by an agent of the secret police.

He had gotten to know Violeta, our school friend who had become a streetwalker. Sad to say, she had sunk lower and lower, had grown very fat, and had let herself be exploited by the pension madams without ever knowing what she was earning or what she was going to eat the next day. Somehow the two of them happened to talk about me one day, and Violeta asked him if she could see me, whether I would have the courage to look upon her as I used to. The proposal to meet her some day soon and talk to her, I naturally accepted with enthusiasm, out of compassion and perhaps curiosity. I began dreaming of the possibility of lending a hand to this lost soul, of finding work for her, of protecting her with my friendship and of saving her. One day I spoke with Maria José and we both laid plans, arranging for

the meeting and preparing our words, which, with
Maria José, would be charitable and moral in tone, and
with me, fraternal and most brief, in order not to hurt
her feelings.

And during our walk that very day, Aluísio told me
that he had suddenly lost sight of Violeta and had just
now learned that she had been shipped off to Pernam-
buco.

This was a deep disappointment for me. I had counted with such certainty upon saving her and fishing her
from that tepid, murky, bottomless pool!

We stayed there walking among the tombs, thoughtfully. Aluísio stopped in front of a sepulcher that we
had always enjoyed looking at, made entirely of black
stone. At the head there was a bronze jardiniere, in
which no one had put a flower all these years.

Aluísio read the inscription once again:

HERE LIES

DONA AMÉLIA SAMPAIO RIBEIRO

WHO DIED AT THE AGE OF NINETEEN

HER MEMORY IS CHERISHED BY HUSBAND AND SON

"Nineteen years old, eh, Guta?—and already dead
and buried, leaving behind her a widower, a son, her
whole life. It almost seems that people in those days
lived faster and wore out more quickly."

No, not at all! Of what importance were her son, her
surviving husband, the life she had lived, compared
with the life ahead of her at nineteen?

To be nineteen is to have the power of youth, whether a girl lives now or in the past, whether she is married or single! When I see pictures of people from other
times, I always think most of the bodies moving be-

neath the hoop skirts and the cutaways, which are as young as our own. Look at my hand: would it be any less my hand at any other time? The same goes for one's heart— She may have left behind a son, a husband, but what we really see here is where a young girl lies buried.

A pauper's funeral procession passed by and interrupted us. It was on its way to the common grave in the remote part of the cemetery, where nothing grows but cockleburs among the humble little crosses painted with pitch and with small white lettering, crooked, faded, the N's and z's backward.

But, why I don't know, I've always felt less sorry for the dead who lie there. They arrive in the charity casket, which has to be returned to the Charity Hospital, and they are placed in direct contact with the ground's clay, dissolved, turned right into humus, into sap, made a part of the earth. The others are shoved into sordid ossuaries and left there, in absolute abandon, turned into something still human, trash, the garbage of life.

In the burial party there were no flowers, no priest, no one weeping.

Maria José met them as they left the chapel. She crossed herself and said some kind of prayer for the repose of that soul.

Afterward she came over to us smiling, held out her hand to each of us, and we left together, holding hands, gently sorrowing, oncoming night hanging heavy over us, so young and so alone the three of us, and life and death all around us, more and more mysterious, unfathomable, and frightening.

Glória's wedding was on a Saturday afternoon and Maria José and I, dressed in pink silk, with flowing skirts and carrying bouquets of tiny satin flowers, shone among the bridesmaids.

Afonso, the bridegroom, wearing the traditional frock coat and spats, and martyred by a stiff collar, was sweating through his shirt front, walking pigeon-toed in his patent-leather shoes and coming up to people to complain in a low voice, bemoaning the fact that he had never suffered so much since graduation day.

Glória was dazzling, a sumptuous and shimmering eminence of satin and tulle, and all of us agreed that she looked lovely.

When I kissed her, after the ceremony, I whispered gaily,

"Now your days as an orphan are over."

Really, they were over so completely that she didn't even hear what I said and, wholly engrossed in these sacrificial rites, she turned to her husband. "Is it time now to go sit on the sofa in the other room?"

In the other living room, the bridegroom's aunt, since the bride had no family, was serving cookies and handing out glasses of warm sweet champagne.

I didn't want anything to eat, barely tasted the wine, and couldn't take my eyes off Glória. Her serenity, her courage in setting out! She seemed to have been ready for this marriage since the day she was born, and the moral side of it apparently didn't occur to her; all she thought of were details of mere form: being careful of her long flowing train, checking her wrist watch of platinum and diamonds (a wedding present from Afonso) to see if it was time to change clothes and get in the automobile, heading for their honeymoon in the mountains. He too, from time to time, took out his pocket watch. He looked lingeringly at his bride; it was obvious that he deeply desired her and was anxious to be gone. Perhaps, too, he was dreaming of the moment he could take his shoes off.

It was the most joyous wedding I have ever seen. At Jandira's the bride was not so lovely, many people were weeping, and there was the grave, almost tragic, note of the unacknowledged mother appearing for the first time. And later the old aunt shouting and embracing the bride, and the bridegroom in a corner, silent and confused.

But not here. All of us kept laughing and eating cookies and making jokes. The unmarried girls advanced on Glória's bridal wreath, the white carnations that Afonso had taken from his wife and was handing out amid laughter.

For Glória, it was as if she had been born that very day, and born without pain, dressed in white silk, loving, loved in return, and in expectation of incomparable delights.

Finally their automobile arrived, all decorated inside and out with orange blossoms, as fragrant, warm, and intimate as a bedroom. Afonso looked toward Glória, who was already dressed in her light traveling coat, and ran to get a small valise, a complicated affair full of brushes, small bottles, and little secret pockets, which was the most important piece of the trousseau.

Afonso hastily said good-bye to everyone, his face all smiles of victory. Glória gave a long embrace to the two of us, who had been her only family there.

Maria José, who kept wiping away tears, bent near her ear and asked if she were afraid. Glória smiled the smile of one who already knows all and feels sorry for the ingenuousness of others.

The open door of the car beckoned to the two lovers. Boldly they got in. Afonso waved a quick good-bye, the chauffeur honked his farewells, someone made a crude joke, and the car was soon far away.

When it was all over and we were in the car going home, Maria José, clinging to her idea, pensively insisted, as she smoothed out the wide folds of her pleats:

"I can't understand how Glória keeps from being afraid."

I laughed. Could she be thinking that everyone was like herself, who never let a boy friend hold her hand, who didn't even consider the prospect of marrying some day because she was afraid to be alone with a man?

"You may say what you like, Guta, but I guarantee that if it were you, you wouldn't be so calm. She gives the appearance of never having done any different-ly—"

I could not remember ever having had any such idea, and I thought that Glória only showed such calm because she lacked our fervent imagination. She was content with the role that luck had brought her and tried only to make a success of things. Up to now she had been the orphan, alone in the world, with only her violin for company. Today, however, she was the wife, the queen, the lover, full of submission and affection. Why dig into the past? The kimonos of flowered silk she wore as an orphaned child no longer fit, nor did those little ermine house slippers, which had appealed so much to us—

"Why should Glória be afraid? Doesn't she like him? Didn't she pick him out? Weren't they always in the corner kissing?"

Maria José took offense, feeling that she was misunderstood, or rather she was irritated by my unsympathetic attitude.

"That's not what I mean. Now it's all different. Before, everybody would look out for them, there was no danger of anything happening. Now— If I were in her place, I would be so afraid and embarrassed, I would die. And so would you!"

I shrugged my shoulders and smiled:

"Me, afraid? If I had done the choosing of my own free will, how could I possibly be afraid?"

But the truth is that I really was afraid. I had brought this all on myself and now I felt fear in my own heart, and suddenly queasy, and anxious to get away.

The automobile was speeding, the rain seemed to be hurtling against us, the driver did not take his eyes off the fan-shaped area which the wiper blade cleared on the windshield, and I huddled in fear, thinking about that other automobile, about Glória's wedding day and what Maria José had said.

Raul held me tight in his arms, making demands in

a voice barely perceptible. I kept taking his hands away, turning my face away from his kisses, sinking down into the cushions, retreating into the farthest corner of the seat.

He had deceived me horribly. His hands outstretched, ever demanding, he wanted only these things, these violent intimacies.

Where were the wonderful things that had been so greatly promised by the look in his eye? Where was the distant man I had seen that first day, standing there smoking in the theater aisle, melancholy, fed up with life? Where were the intoxicating words I was expecting, the revelations of a dream world, the divine stupor abolishing all my awareness, the love that would be different, the caresses without form or weight?

Only those hands, that mouth, his nervous little body, creaking, feverish, voracious.

What madness for me to have gone out with him! How had I ever agreed to this ride, what did I expect?

The suggestiveness of a rainy day, when everything is misty and clandestine through the fog, his invitation, my own uncontrolled impulses—

The road had become ruts of mud which were flowing with torrents, the car skidded, the driver kept applying the foot pedal, braking violently, missing holes.

Think now what would happen if the car turned over, if it plunged off the cliff there, and the two of us were hurt, perhaps one of us killed—

And the scandal, and we in the hospital, and his wife, and what my stepmother would say when she found out—

Now Raul was kissing my eyes, my hair, and again my lips. His hands kept advancing, he becoming more and more eager, more and more daring. I kept repulsing him, and I felt my skin turn harsh upon contact with his hands, as if even it were alarmed.

Truly the fury of his desire exceeded by far the measure of my love for him—and I felt no need for such a thing, barely understanding the reason for his straining face, for this urgency that made him shake.

Agonizingly I did my best to hold him off, to bring him back to mere kisses, to words, to gentle words: "You're frightening me, Raul. Don't forget about the driver. Are you out of your mind, Raul?"

And he spoke softly, breathing his words, "Why don't you want to? Why are you afraid?"

He released me for a moment, tapped the driver on the shoulder, and gave the order to go back. The man went ahead for a bit, finally turned off, maneuvered dangerously in the mud, and made the car retrace its earlier route between palm groves and lagoons full of water lilies.

And once more Raul held me close, whispering pleasantly, as if having discovered a solution, "Let's go to my studio, now. No one will see you and you can leave right away."

I stiffened as he held me and got as far away from him as I could. "No, not a chance! It was stupid of me to come here in the first place! Now you want me—"

He meanwhile was insistent, renewed his violent caresses, pushed his hands through the openings in my sleeves, in the neck of my dress. And I, now more than ever, felt and knew perfectly that I did not want to.

"I'm not going. You're a fool! Let me go or I'll get out right here, in the middle of the rain."

At last he seemed to understand, and turned me loose, in fury, surprise, humiliation. "So, what did you want me to do? What were you thinking? Did you think that

I'm a plaything, a puppet dressed like a painter to pay you compliments?"

That was it, oh Lord, that was more or less what I had thought and what I had perhaps expected!

"You're not a child any longer. You want to be independent, you say you're free, so why are you afraid?" And his words kept coming brutally, insolently, wantonly like his kisses before, and they came from the same impulse.

"—you wanted 'literature,' just the words of love— Sure, when you let yourself go, it's with the young fellows, with that silly student who's so full of theories— Me, I'm just the 'painter' as far as you're concerned—"

And I kept trying to talk and explain my way of loving and the way I supposed he loved me, and, despite everything, I was getting lost in repetitions of that forbidden verb, no longer able to order my feelings in the confusion of settling of accounts, at that moment in which he demanded I pay for my imprudent fantasies with my body.

"Love? You want to talk to me about love?"

And he seized me by the shoulders, pulled me to him, and said brutally:

"Then you didn't understand from the very first that you would end up being my mistress?"

Perhaps this was logical for him and for everyone else. But it was not so for me. And I did not want to be his mistress. I could see that I did not want to, I was afraid, and I was unable to feel desire, that kind of desire. Raul's theatrical speech struck me as ridiculous and false and brought to mind Carmen and Don José and his dark figure on the half-lighted stage.

The road through the carnauba groves had come to an end, the rain was now but a mist, and the car was pulling into a street that was near the end of the streetcar line.

Raul moved away from me and composed himself.

I picked up my purse, my beret, my notes from English class that were strewn and crumpled on the seat. I straightened the collar of my blouse, smoothed my disheveled hair, and said:

"Have him stop at the end of the line. I want to take the streetcar. It's best for no one to see us together."

Raul obeyed without speaking, got out of the car, and helped me courteously. Discreetly, the driver didn't even turn around, as if he were another motor in the car, without vision or conscience.

The streetcar was waiting at the end of the line, and I got on, as numb and heroic as if I had come out of a battle. His car was already disappearing in the distance, and I could still feel on my arms and neck the rough warmth of his hands.

The streetcar began to pick up speed, its curtains insecurely fastened, and the mist that came in with the gusts of wind little by little refreshed and pacified me.

I got home and only then felt distress at what I had done; I was distressed by the resentment I felt when I left him, and what hurt me most, certainly, was the unexpected denouement.

I saw that everything was over and I suddenly longed

for the Seine, his fascinating stories, his words of love, the tender pride I felt in being loved, in seeing his eyes seeking me in the midst of everyone else, anxiously seeking for me as for a light.

What did I know about the nature of man, about what love really was? Now I blamed myself, thought over Raul's accusations, and began to see myself through his eyes as an inconsistent, incoherent, silly girl who wanted to play at love with a man, with a man who knew all too well what this meant.

Suddenly I wanted to make amends, to redo the whole thing.

I wrote him a long letter, in which I tried to set forth my conception of love, the only kind that could exist between us. He, a married man, I, an immature girl— I certainly did love him, how could he doubt it? Would I have let things reach the stage they did, if I hadn't?

But oh how easy it was to write, how moving and intoxicating it was to say these words of love, far from the reach of his hands, his hot, hungry breath.

I filled four pages. I wrote feverishly, struggling to put my romance back together, desperately clinging to its debris, stricken with longing for my lost emotions, the sweet excitement of those first days, the tall chair where I posed, my painter, his somber, suggestive studio.

I never heard from him.

Some days later he sent the painting, in a large red frame. All his deception and bitterness seemed to have carried into the portrait, into the sad smile with downcast lips which he had accentuated, into my dim, dull, lusterless eyes.

The deliveryman who brought it said nothing and left not even a card, not even the least little message.

It was hard for me to get used to the idea of losing Raul. People never accept an event when and as it happens; I am not sure whether anyone has thought about this before, but it has always seemed to me that in order to become truly real an event must happen subjectively within us, after having happened objectively in the real world.

I had the idea of going to the studio to thank him for the portrait. I went unaccompanied and expected that I might perhaps find Raul alone. And meanwhile I was certain that I would repel him if he should start taking too many liberties again. No doubt what I wanted was to give my own desire one more chance, to be swept once more into temptation, to look into his ravenous, suppliant eyes, to feel the touch of his hands, to have the frightening homage of his desire, to begin again the thrilling contest of demand and refusal.

But there were people in the studio, three girls and a boy—his regular drawing students.

A tall fat girl with enormous arms, heavily mascaraed deep-set eyes, and a thin line of eyebrows arching in admiration high upon her forehead was beaming and ecstatically contemplating Raul, while he, in his white smock, holding palette in one hand and with the other brandishing a long brush, was making a series of blotches on the canvas, explaining the fundamental combinations of colors. Next to the fat girl sat two other young ladies, one a blond with a tired expression, and, her companion, a small, dark, and rather plain girl. Raul, however, was not watching them, nor was he watching the boy, who was busily drawing concentric circles on paper, in which he proceeded to write: green, blue, orange, red.

Raul's sure instinct drew him to the other brunette, as he cultivated the warm and tender admiration which he read in her dark eyes; to this end he was utilizing the best of his charms, those with which he had captivated me, interspersing classroom explanations with romantic anecdotes from his days as a *rapin* in Paris, speaking in short, precise phrases that were full of wit and simple charm.

I stood there for a while, leaning on the stairway banisters, listening to him talk. With his back to me, Raul could not see me, and if he heard my steps he gave no heed to whom it might be, perhaps imagining some tardy student.

And I heard him repeat the same stories with which he had bewitched me, like someone seeing the rerun of a film, expecting, foreseeing each gesture, each expression, each smile.

I knew when he was going to underline his words with a tired and doleful droop of his lips, recounting how he went hungry in Europe; or when he would wave the brush with broad strokes in the air, to tell how Uni, the Swedish girl who had loved him, had the peculiarity of thus painting small pictures with large background masses of color.

The big girl with the fleshy arms kept listening to him in ecstasy; she too at that moment was in Paris, painted with him, loved with him, lived the same restless Bohemian life. And I, a spectator now that the role of the enraptured young thing was being played by another, could see, one after another, all the tricks from which my own infatuation had arisen. I was a bit pained by it all; I was jealous of the other girl, humiliatingly and violently jealous, but I was lucid, tremendously cold and lucid.

I waited for a pause, raised my voice, and said hello to him. Raul turned around brusquely, and I got the impression that he was displeased to feel that he had thus been spied upon in the midst of his magic—and particularly by me.

But he quickly concealed his annoyance, had me sit down, introduced me to the young ladies, was attentive to my thanks, and took modest exception to my warm words of appreciation. Still in a daze of happiness, the large girl kept letting her smile turn from him to me. I asked her if Raul was not going to do her portrait.

"Yes, yes, a modern painting, with neutral colors, in pastel tones—"

With chagrin, Raul changed the subject. Outwardly I was all smiles.

I did not accept the liqueur which he offered me, stood up, on the pretext of not wishing to interrupt his class any longer, and said my good-byes.

He accompanied me to the door, walking down the stairway with me. When I was about to leave he took my hand firmly and muttered furiously:

"Anyone seeing your disapproving little manner and faultfinding smile would think that I'm the one who has offended you, that I'm the one to blame—"

I took my hand away.

"No— I just wanted to see, from the wings, how you operate. What a marvelous illusionist you are! The poor girl is already in a daze, more in a daze than I ever was."

And now on the sidewalk, as I drew away, I put in:

"What I regret is that you didn't pick out a prettier successor for me— It would be less disagreeable now."

He may have replied, but I was already quite a distance away. He bit his lip, stood for a moment at the door, and watched me walk away.

I walked fast, until I felt that he was out of sight. I stopped at the corner and caught my breath for an instant, looking at the dahlias and lilies in Cathedral Square. I dried my eyes carefully, and touched up the rouge on my cheeks, because I had wept, naturally.

I began to get depressed and nervous. At work I was impatient, and I felt lonely, with no one to turn to. At night I started getting back my old desire to kill myself. An almost lyrical desire, with no possibility of realization, certainly, but which once more would occupy my long sleepless hours; I would see the poison in the bottle, imagine the dull thud of the knife, and then the joy of gradually expiring, of feeling my life slowly running out, like blood dripping from a slashed wrist.

To me, young thing that I was, who at an age for

dreams and hopes no longer had either dreams or hopes and had reached unfathomable desperation, completely alone in an immense world devoid of destiny and solution, death seemed to be port, limit, tranquility. The difficult part, however, is to explain myself properly, because the theme in itself already bears an age-old burden of banality and is a kind of commonplace of human grief, whether actually experienced or literary.

In self-destruction what always terrified me, then as now, is the tragicomical publicity that attends it. And always having felt such a profound need for death, I have never failed to be horrified by the idea of also making a spectacle for the onlookers who remain, and of the horrid sensationalism of the act, which amounts to a posthumous immodesty.

And because I could not forget this, I then considered discreet ways of dying of unsuspected cause, "the perfect crime" of detective stories: the poison that leaves no trace, the careless stroller run down by the train, the solitary bather caught by the surf and never brought back.

It was a lucid delirium and for that very reason the more dangerous and morbid.

I felt as if I were drunk, drunk on something toxic and evil, made up of small woes, of all my disillusionment, and of my small errors and failures, something which heightened, magnified, and deformed imagination.

By night everything grows in size and terrifies when seen from within one's insomnia. Everything looks hostile, like a submarine world full of viscous things and treacherous sharp edges, of suckers and of spines. Everything is invisible, inimical, imprecise. The soul becomes infected with shadow and sees only in terms of black.

How they pain us, these little daily humiliations remembered in the silence of the solitary night! And also how we struggle for vengeance, how implacably, furiously, we crush the enemy forces that surround us, how we battle, how we conquer!

By day, whether it was interesting or not, I was occupied by my work, and by the momentum of life: books, movies, Luciano, General.

Glória wrote infrequent, superficial, hasty letters; in her happiness she was detaching herself from us.

Maria José, also distraught and depressed, had been complaining much of late about her father's hopeless case, discussing fearfully the future of his children, who were being raised without guidance in that house without a man, where they lacked at least the prestige of a deceased and virtuous father, as true orphans have, to get them started in life. And she prayed and prayed more and more wildly, praying like someone wailing in despair; she calloused her knees with kneeling, disorganized her days in hours of worship, ran from class to receive blessing, took communion, and went to mass every morning.

I had been caught up in my relationship with Raul at the beginning of one of my own periods of depression. It was an interruption, a passionate diversion. It was all over suddenly, however, with our unexpected breaking off. And after the brief moment of agitation and activity, my mental crisis continued from where it had stopped, or rather, had continued motionlessly, at a standstill.

After Raul's withdrawal, Aluísio came around more often, as if to avail himself of the place left vacant by the other.

He used to come to our house almost every day, chat a while in Dona Júlia's parlor, bring books, and romp with General and Luciano, who were always running around at my heels.

Maria José liked him very much. They used to have furious discussions about religion; he, for some reason had a special interest (which I called jealousy) in destroying in her the tender devotion that drew her to the most ingenuous and childlike saints of the hagiology: Saint Luís Gonzaga, Teresinha, the Guardian Angel. Not to mention all the angels! Of the entire dogma, this was what most irritated him, what seemed to him most absurd and inconceivable:

"Angels? Why should there be angels? Can't you see they're only a joke? That they are an affront to the most elementary common sense? If they are pure spirit, why did they sin? And if they can sin, why are they superior to us and beyond the risk of heaven and hell and of the earth's miseries? They're something like God's servants, or musicians, singing and playing their harps."

Patiently, Maria José would explain:

"They are the messengers of God, Aluísio, the intermediaries between Him and men. They are indispensable to the harmony between heaven and earth."

"That's what I said, servants, servants of Our Lord! The inventions of a slave-holding society, which you all endorse!"

But he would calm down right away, take his seat, for he had stood up and gesticulated in the heat of discussion, and smilingly conclude:

"Speaking of angels, I can think of only one; I know only one: you, Josie."

"What about Guta?" she replied.

Aluísio, however, would shake his head:

"Guta can't be an angel. She belongs to those the Scriptures call "the daughters of man.""

That last night, Aluísio came into our room to see Raul's painting, which I had hung at the head of my bed.

And he thought the portrait was really beautiful, discovering in it countless subtleties of expression that I had never been able to perceive. But in praising the painting he never praised the painter; he even went so far as to say:

"He paints well. But one gets the impression that, in him, art is not a spiritual need but a manual skill. It doesn't come from intelligence or sensibility, just from diligence and patience."

I smiled, but without comment. Aluísio had taken this dislike for the man suddenly, after accompanying me several times to the posing sessions. He himself was the one who introduced me to Raul, amid enthusiastic exclamations; now, however, he only referred to him with ironic reservations, calling him "your painter."

That night, as he kept this up, I interrupted him:

"That's enough, Aluísio. I've had a quarrel with him. I've lost a lot of my illusions."

And I didn't have the courage to admit my own part in it; I felt that it would be humiliating myself too much to tell how I had given my consent, how I had brought it all about. I lied cowardly in response to Aluísio's questions:

"He was a little too forward, I got disgusted, pushed him away, and we quarreled."

Aluísio was satisfied with that, and I allowed my ambiguity to stand, shamefully. And now, after seeing the picture, we were in the parlor, silent, each thinking his own thoughts.

Aluísio kept smoking and looking at me. I could tell that he wanted to speak, but he couldn't or wouldn't say what was on the tip of his tongue.

He got up, stood leafing through some magazines that I had left on a coffee table, sat down again, and once more started looking at me, his cigarette in hand, as before. Finally he said, "Today you're hard to figure out!"

I smiled. "Quit talking in riddles, silly boy. You're the one who's hard to figure out."

He too smiled, but sadly. "No, Guta, my trouble is that I'm a flop."

And I thought to myself: imagine how disillusioned, how disgusted, how angry he would be if he knew what I am thinking now. Because, at that moment I was still remembering the true history of what had gone on between Raul and me, our stupid, shattered romance. He, however, had no hint of any of this, fortunately, nor had he any idea of my own woes. He was thinking of his own, of course, because he spoke again.

"If people could only tell, Guta—"

Maria José came in with the coffee-maker.

The conversation broken off, we dropped our musing and confiding.

When he left, Aluísio held my hand in his longer than usual, and his hands seemed hot and rather shaky.

Is that the way things really seemed, at that moment, or was it suggested by what happened later?

Because on the morning of the following day, while I was still in my room reading, Maria José arrived with the unexpected news, as cruel and unexpected then as the account I am giving here: that Aluísio had taken several tablets of corrosive sublimate and was near death.

There was talk about a letter. A letter addressed to his father, in the backlands, which his uncle had found and read.

No one else had seen that letter, just the uncle. Apparently it spoke of me. Apparently it alluded to an unhappy love affair, to an uncomprehended passion which had brought him to that end.

And Maria José concluded,

"Everyone says that it was because of you."

I was vaguely afraid of something like that. But I couldn't keep from protesting with a hurt cry:

"Me? Only yesterday he was here, and you saw him too! He didn't say a thing, he had nothing against anyone. He never said a word to me! Why should it have been on my account?"

Yes, why on my account? There had never been any love scenes between us. Perhaps I might have guessed that he was in love with me, like some schoolboy who loves a mature woman. But just a guess and nothing more. And then there were his hands, hot and shaky, the evening before, and the personal confession he had merely begun.

Maria José went on:

"Yesterday when he left here, he met up with friends. They had some drinks and Aluísio, they say, had more than anyone else, got rather wild, and offered some queer toasts. He said a lot of outlandish things, talked about a sphinx, about a woman 'who left him only two alternatives: death or ridicule'."

The boys paid no attention and did not take his threats seriously. Whenever he had a few drinks, he would get wound up and start talking about suicide. This time he got so drunk, finally, that the others took him home in an automobile. He was put in bed fully clothed and still talking nonsense.

When did he get up? Where did he find the poison? No one knows. His uncle, who sleeps in the room next to his, waked in the early morning hours to hear some-one gasping; it was he, and he wanted to die.

He was still gasping for breath when I went to see him at noon. They gave me entry to the house, as if I myself were the angel of death. No one said a word to me, not even a harsh word, not even an unfriendly ges-ture; but they had a way of making room for me, of looking at me, as if I were a murderess, as if that boy with his burned and withered mouth who lay moaning in bed, had been hurt by my hands.

There was no dramatic recognition, no scene. My throat was feeling tight and stiff, but I didn't cry; he didn't recognize me, or if he did, he didn't care, no doubt thinking solely and inexorably about death, his own stupid, idiotic death that was already seizing him and dragging him off, poor unhappy child laid low by a dangerous toy.

The others kept looking silently at me with curiosity. Did they perchance think I was going to fall on my knees and beg for forgiveness?

I didn't give it a thought. I didn't feel to blame and why should I? It was he who hurt me, dragged me with him when he plunged down into the abyss.

By what right had he so brutally intruded upon my tranquility? Why had he brought along this drama-filled bedroom, these grief-stricken relatives, and come to die in my life?

Up to that moment he had been almost a stranger, just somebody to pal around with. Suddenly he had laid hold of me, stripped me naked, and tied me to the head of his deathbed at the mercy of everyone's cruelty, as to a whipping post.

He was sobbing now, harsh, unconscious, mechanical sobs. His hands would move and his mouth convulsively contract between heaves. Pitiful, pitiful child. He looked like a little boy in bed, a little boy dying. His hair in ringlets on his sweaty forehead, his nose in sharp relief, frantically inhaling like a drowning thing.

It was so painful to see him thus isolated in his death throes, now detached from us all, unaware of me, un-aware of anyone, struggling all alone as if nothing else in this world existed except him and his anguish!

I put the knuckles of my fingers in my mouth and began biting back my own sobs.

I stepped behind the head of the bed; for an instant I forgot the people watching me, the inimical faces around me, and I let my own tears blind me, relieve me a bit of the terrible weight that had been oppressing me since Maria José had come in with the news.

When I took my eyes off his perspiring brow, his restless hands, his rumbling chest, the crumpled shirt of the previous day still hanging on a chair, together with his checkered tie which only yesterday—and once more turned my thoughts to the others, they looked at me less hostilely, with a certain pitying curiosity; now I felt they were less my enemies. Perhaps they thought that I, at last, had become imbued with my role and was weeping.

Poor, pathetic boy. Everything was ordinary and cheap and lacking in grandeur. He may have thought of some sublime gesture, his drunkenness aiding his dream; perhaps he had imagined to appear great in my eyes, in everyone's eyes, suddenly full of the awesome prestige, the overwhelming majesty of death.

And he had forgotten about the setting, forgotten about the details.

He had written the letter, no doubt filled with its terrible accusations, or with ironical laments. But now they had fastened a handkerchief around his jaw, a handkerchief with a little knot on top, a humble, ridiculous little knot. They had dressed him and put his shoes on him, and the toes of his shoes emerged strangely from among the poppies withering at his feet. Tallow from the candles was dripping down, staining the wooden floor in big greasy spots.

One could see the nails holding the gold trimming that adorned the coffin, stretching the black cloth tight; the entire staging of death, exhibited in the light of day, was false, bare, and cheap, like a theater set.

His aunt kept blowing her nose and repeating for the

other women the text of the telegram sent to the family.

Young girls came with wreaths, older women with rosaries in hand, and they all knelt around the coffin and prayed.

What words can convey the impression of irrevocably broken and impossible communication, of absolutely useless action, of distance, of severance, and of parting all ties that we are given by the presence of the dead?

Why do they make still another gesture, why do they kiss his cold forehead, why the flowers, why do they stand around keeping fearsome vigil, looking upon decomposition, watching the separation get worse and worse, seeing one who meant everything to them— lover, son, father, mother, brother, or sister—become, moment by moment, more indifferent and remote, more unknown, more intrusive and terrible?

Why overcome our fear, our instinctive horror? Indeed only fear and horror are right.

I felt sorrow and immense pity, but not remorse as Maria José and the others expected. Rather, I had maintained my original impression of near-hatred toward him—if not hatred, at least grievance. It seemed to me that I had been betrayed by Aluísio, that he had gone against his words and gestures of friendship, his confidences, the trust that existed between us, using me thus to help him put on his tragic and sensational act.

He had seized upon me treacherously, and had pitilessly turned me over to everyone's curiosity, to the terrible gossiping of all those who knew us and took pleasure in making up cruel and impossible stories about us.

Especially, what right did he have to impose such mourning and grief upon me, and, just because he had drunk too much with some of his friends, what right did he have to wound my spirit?

Poor boy, he became so serious-looking, with his face all full of pain and surprise! He didn't see me, he didn't recognize me. And to say that he had killed himself over me! But where were his words of supreme, passionate, final confession?

He died in agony and silence, with no further concern for anything, except perhaps his desperate defense, between sobs and hoarse gasps, against the poison that was burning his body and blinding his eyes.

As for the supposed letter, I was never able to see it. Did it at least exist? Why everyone's insistence that it was my fault? He never said anything to me, to me or to anyone else. Only the eyes and the unfriendly whispers of those people kept telling me so. In truth, I was *his* victim, the victim of the suicide who now lay in peace, who was no longer aware of what he had done.

Aluísio's head was full of absurdities, and he was always imagining strange things, creating conflicts and dramas. He attributed importance only to his own imagination, and any given fact of the moment impressed him only after being mulled over and transformed in his mind. This is what really killed him, not I. If he liked me, why didn't he say so? For lack of opportunity? He had plenty of opportunities. We went

around together, and talked a great deal in endless conversations. One evening the two of us spent a long time
together in the parlor, leaning over the table, leafing
through the same book. Why didn't he speak out then,
say something, at least by implication? I even led him
on a bit that evening, impelled by some perverse instinct. I let my arm touch his; he remained serious
and unmoved, like an innocent child. If he was in love
with me, as they maintain, why did he not try something at that moment? Too timid? And how about
his confiding in me? He used to talk about his secret
troubles, about his irregular life as a student, even
about the women he went with. And I would encourage
him to speak openly with me and took an interest in
the affairs of his morbid, complicated heart, and of a
brain that was too full.

If, then, someone was to blame, if someone did kill
him, it was that feverish brain of his, not I.

Meanwhile, everyone was surprised that I had not
put on mourning, like a widow.

All his aunt could call me was "that daughter of
Satan"; she told everybody how I had seduced the boy,
how I had led him into evil and insanity, making him
read vile books, blaspheming the saints, taking walks
with him even in the cemetery, the two of us lost in
endless conversation. And finally I had come to see
Aluísio die, had stood by his bed with steely eyes, without a tear, without a gesture of friendship or repentance,
while the poor lad now longing for death kept his eye
on me, still under my spell, still begging for all the
things I mutely denied him.

"Why, she didn't even shed a tear, not a one!"

And the truth is that my eyes kept filling up with water all the time, and my suffering, sorrowing heart was like something stepped on.

And at night, in my hours of insomnia, that were now more terrible than ever, my sleeplessness was filled with those torments, with my secret, silent weeping.

I quit looking at the world, which had always before seemed to me so lovely—the sky, the landscape, the flowers. I acquired a horror of roses—flowers to bedeck the dead, burial flowers, made to be smelled inside coffins and on top of tombs.

I was afraid to read; every book is an evocation of tragedy. There are so many dead young men in story-book pages; and young men who are alive, who can still laugh and smoke, hold the hands of their girls, and read passages out loud, how they do indeed love books!

My dejection began to concern Maria José.

"You're so depressed these days, Guta, so downcast! You always were precocious; and you're already an old maid at your age. Why don't you ask for leave and go to Rio? I'm going to write your stepmother about this."

True enough, I myself felt irritable and bitter inside, full of preoccupations and prone to sudden tears. I hung on to the idea of the trip. I wrote Papa and got the money. It wasn't easy to write him with this request; there was no intimate and affectionate correspondence between us; he never used to write because he had a

horror of letters. It was with Godmother that I exchanged monthly news in terms of friendly formality,
telling about my health and the heat, about shoes for
the little ones, and medicines that were at times un-
available in Crato. A few lines in a large hand, filling
three-quarters of a tablet page.

Fortunately, however, Papa understood my need for
a change of horizons and my desire to see a bit of the
world. They had heard in Crato the story of Aluísio's
suicide, naturally confused and exaggerated. Replying
to the letter from Maria José, Godmother told how
Papa, when he heard the news, spent two days without
speaking to anyone, smoking, and striding up and down
the porch, his face grim. Without saying a word he listened to the message from Maria José that Godmother
had relayed to him; and the following day he had some
animals sold and sent me the money in an envelope
with a hasty, affectionate card: "To my darling daughter, for her trip, with love and kisses from Papa." My
stepmother sent me a woolen scarf as protection against
the cold weather and a page and a half of advice on
morals and colds.

I arranged to take three months' leave away from the
office; Maria José and two fellows who worked with
us accompanied me to the gangplank.

Luciano went along too, and I tried to stir his feelings, talking about our separation and missing each
other. He, however, didn't even hear me and turned
an absent-minded cheek to me for a kiss, interested as
he was in the launches, the cranes, the ships, and their
flags.

So I went aboard, with no emotional farewells, all
alone, vaguely commended by Dona Júlia to the care
of acquaintances who were traveling to the South.

I had never been aboard ship in my life. To me, a ship was a fairy palace, sailing the seas with its cargo of delightful people and pleasures beyond compare. Everything white, the polished metal gleaming, just as in the movies. Young men from foreign shores in white flannel, telling stories of far-off lands; an orchestra at meals, bars, cocktail parties, ballrooms, women in low-cut dresses smoking— Everything that I had never seen, that I had never dared desire in my unfailingly austere and pleasureless life.

And naturally I found none of this.

I was seasick the entire trip. In port I never left the ship because I didn't know anyone ashore and had not made any friends aboard, always stuck in my state-room, perspiring, dizzy, nauseated. Only in Recife did I perk up a bit and take a few timid turns around the pier, afraid of going farther, of getting lost in the city and missing the boat.

Aboard, how vile things smelled, how hot and inse-cure everything was! How my head ached and my eyes hurt and what an awful dismal hole my stateroom was! One had merely to open the door to feel the warm draft that came from within, as from a dirty furnace; and I could scarcely manage to drag myself to my berth; I would drop down on the hard mattress that smelled of mildew and disinfectant and remain there in a kind of coma, without body heat or heartbeat, until some kind-ly steward came to my aid.

If the ship stopped I would come to life, put on bet-ter clothes, and go out on deck.

But everyone would already have left the ship to go ashore, just an old gentleman sick with beriberi remain-ing on deck, stretched out in his deck chair, with his old-maid daughter at his side. And I would sit down too, or lean on the rail gloomily watching the few passers-by who ventured on the wharf, the cranes creaking as they loaded and unloaded, the longshoremen as they slept in the scant shade of the warehouses.

The first days in Rio were days of tiredness, of noise and tedium. A particular kind of tedium, a sort of tedium in motion, relentlessly monotonous, like the steady roar of a machine.

The tedium of feeling myself useless and alone, inoperative in the midst of everyone else's agitation, without reference point or affective link with anyone, astray into the midst of a strange crowd.

Incessant noise, people and more people, a furious surge dizzily impelling automobiles and men on the street, the street vendors, the buses racing madly as if to rescue from a conflagration the remote places whose names they carry on placards and that remind me of poems. And even at the small boardinghouse where I had taken a room, the disconcerting noise was propagated through gossipy, shrill dinner-table conversations, couched in irreverent slang which mixed me up: through streetcars that passed by in a steady stream, shaking the whole house; through the movie-struck colored maid who made her cleaning rounds singing popular tunes in a soprano voice; through the telephone loudly and indefatigably summoning the boys of the house, one by one; through the boys themselves, who elbowed each other in the mornings at the bathroom door, ate their steak and potatoes at a dash at lunch-time, and bestowed loud smacks (everything was loud, terribly loud!) on the pink cheeks of Dona Adelina, the Portuguese landlady: she would wipe her face with the bottom of her apron and gaily call them "rapscallions."

I had been recommended to that house by Dona Júlia. Living there were her sister and her husband, who was an army doctor, an asthmatic, high-strung man given to violent discussions, which were frightening because of his deep, thundering voice.

He would argue about anything: about the theater and morals, about agriculture and mathematics, but especially about history. He vehemently expressed his unlimited admiration for Henry IV and the Edict of Nantes, Danton, the Marquis of Pombal ("Sebastião José de Carvalho e Mello, Count of Oeiras and Marquis of Pombal"), and Floriano Peixoto ("How shall they be received, Marshal?" "Mow 'em down!"). He also admired Camille Flammarion. In literature he was very fond of Júlio Dantas, through some mysterious and frivolous affinity. And, after seeing him at the table arguing in stentorian tones about speeches in the Convention or about the expulsion of the Jesuits, it was uproariously funny to hear him recite in his mellif-luous voice, winking a devilish eye and smiling beneath his yellow moustache, the gallant vulgarities of his poet.

Having been notified by his sister-in-law, he came to meet me at the dock, arm in arm with his stout and placid wife, so different from Dona Júlia that no one would take them for sisters: one, worn out and old-looking, from cooking and filling lunch pails; the other, smiling and well-groomed, with a fox fur around her shoulders.

As my mentors, they were comfortable, amiable, and indifferent. They never bothered me and let me leave the house alone, at any hour, without raising their eyebrows or criticizing. Dona Alice gave me advice solely with respect to dress, footwear, and cut-rate stores, and she was most helpful. The Major liked modern women and favored feminine independence; his ideal type of woman was a sort of sexless suffragette, who would knock down any man who tried to flirt with her on the street, who could earn a good salary in an office, and who could speak at least three languages.

Meanwhile, it didn't take me long to become acclimated. In a week I was already acquainted with the downtown area, knew my way around, and had made friends. And now I was taking part in the dinner-table conversations and could smile at boys' friendly overtures.

I chatted especially with Dr. Isaac, a Roumanian with red hair and large white hands, slow and grave of speech, with a picturesque archaic accent that reminded you of dead languages being spoken. He was a doctor, had come to Brazil the year before, and was studying in order to validate his diploma. He liked to tell me about his native country, and he talked about people and places with harmonious names like those of Greek heroes.

Some quiet evenings he and I would happen to stay in the parlor after all the others had left. Only the Major would be dozing in his easy chair, and Dona Adelina knitting by a floor lamp, with a shade as somber and horrendous as a rain hat.

Isaac then would go to his room, bring in a package of records, remove from the phonograph the carnival-type march that the boys had left playing when they went out; and he would put on for me—perhaps also for himself, to bring back memories—old gypsy songs, full of wailing violins and musical onomatopoeias, and Russian melodies, doleful and passionate, whose stories of separated lovers and tragic deaths he smilingly translated.

Dona Adelina, slowly nodding her head, would accompany the rhythm of the music; the Major woke up now and then and broke his private silence with words of approbation.

And I listened entranced, as I slowly took possession of Isaac's remote world and saw its gentle landscapes, which he had evoked for me: its flocks, its shepherds, primitive and rustic like those in the Bible, the quiet villages, the lovely Balkan sky, the high craggy mountains appearing in the distance.

He would make me tell too about my native Cariri, which was as exotic and distant from Rio as the needles of the Carpathians. About Juàzeiro and the mystics, the unfinished church at Hôrto, rising out of the top of a naked hill of rock like a ruin from other ages; beside the church, the tile-covered shed full of votive offerings; and the atrium paved with stones, on which the pilgrims leave their footprints, in bloody traces.

I told him about my rides with Papa, in the mornings, during the rainy season: the horses would get lost in the cane brakes, along the lakes, or in the rough tangled brush, and always we had on the horizon the great mass of the Araripe, blue and constant like a shore line.

Isaac and I started going out together. He took me to

his favorite places in the city: to Arpoador Beach, with the waves beating furiously on the great rocks, where one could feel remote from the world, with only the sea and the stones, like a lighthouseman in his tower; or on leisurely walks along the waterfront, in the late hours of afternoon, when the water starts to turn dark and sad and the European sailors leave their ships in little groups—ingenuous faces, heavy of foot, heading for the city and for the Mangue district.

He taught me to enjoy the small cafés, especially a little corner place, with glass doors, that was hidden by the enormous bulk of a skyscraper just opposite. We used to spend whole afternoons in there talking, each one telling whatever was on his mind, discussing, talking about books, medicine, about ourselves and others. Then by nightfall, when we left, it would be cold in the street and the winter mist would be darkening the lights along the avenue. Isaac took me by the arm, I buttoned my wrap up tight, and with him leading me, we dashed madly through the midst of buses and automobiles, without ever really knowing where we were supposed to take the streetcar.

Shortly I, who had been tirelessly making myself take the classical excursions—Quinta, Pão de Açúcar, Tijuca, Corcovado, began centering my preferences in Isaac, and he finally came to epitomize for me all the interest of the city, of the early mornings, of the luminous middays, of the nights in which we wandered all by ourselves, unknown and happy, among the streets, squares, and groves that for us had no names.

One night we took a bus and came upon a beach—distant Leblon, with its unending sands.

Here was the wilderness, the primitive world, the lost island, solitude. The waves covered up the sound of the streetcars that passed behind us in the distant city on which we were turning our backs.

At first we stood motionless, together but each one alone, seeing with his own eyes the violent beauty of the heavens, the night, and the ocean. Afterward each of us began to place the other in the landscape, and, oppressed and restless, to feel a greater need for the other, for a more specific tenderness.

We sat down on the sand, Isaac put his arm around me and, suddenly at peace and happy, I did not move away from him. A cold winter wind was blowing from the ocean; we pulled our coats tighter about us and drew ourselves closer to each other. His cold hands came together within the folds of my coat. And it was good to be in his arms, to feel his heart beating so close to me, his mouth playing softly over my hair, over my eyes. Finally I gained that impression of felicity and calm that I had always thought impossible, unattainable, in the vacuum of those former nights, when, in long imaginings, I nurtured my desire to die. I simply stopped at that point. I did not think, I did not dream, I wished nothing, I let myself be as I was, passive and immobile.

He roused before I did, released me, stood up, looked at his watch, and turned completely around, as if to orient himself. I too stood up, somewhat dizzily, without knowing why the marvelous moment had ended. I accompanied him, and we made our way back to the paved road, to the end of the lighted street that linked up with our desert.

On the streetcar, which was almost empty, we sat in the rearmost seat, hand in hand, I smiling at him, Isaac silently snuggling me to his big angular shoulder, my face touching the coarse cloth of his coat.

In the middle of the trip back—it was almost an hour by streetcar—it began to rain and little splashes of mist hit us in the face. Isaac wanted to close the curtain, but I wouldn't consent and stayed his hand. The drops of cold water hitting me in the face expanded my world of happiness and took me back to the times when Mama was alive—to the shower baths in the yard and our laughter, and my heart leaping with joy. It was the same joy now. The rain, the smell of the rain, the cool of the drops of water, Mama romping with me, so lovely and happy, her hair dripping down her back, her feet treading the little pebbles on the ground, with me shouting all around her, clutching her, embracing her, breathless with happiness.

It was as if Isaac, through the miracle of his presence, of his arm around my shoulder, had restored me to my childhood, to pure naked joy, as the wet wind struck me in the mouth and eyes.

Behind their iron fences, moist gardens were giving off a rustic fragrance of earth, of damp leaves, of flowers opening. Isaac held me tight, the streetcar sped ahead blindly, without seeking its way through the mist and the night. We didn't speak, just laughed, squeezed each other's hands, and pressed closer to each other.

When I got home, I found a letter from Maria José on my night stand. The extension of my leave had not been granted. The only way was without pay. And

naturally my funds must be about exhausted. Did I
still have enough for two more weeks? she asked in a
happy vein. Perhaps it would be best to pack my things,
leave this easy life behind, and get back on the job.
Luciano asked me to bring him an airplane that would
fly by itself. General had disappeared from home for
three days and had finally come back, dirty, dragging
one leg, and so hungry that his stomach had nearly
shrunk up and disappeared. "That person" (her father)
had embarked for the North; the word was that he was
taking his wife and child. Suddenly showing up on a
street corner, he had told his daughter good-bye. He had
left in her hand, just before he started to go, a heavy
diamond-studded gold ring.

Another piece of news: Aluísio's mother had finally
died. Everyone said that her son's suicide had caused
her death. We, however, knew very well that she had
always been consumptive and run-down.

And what was I doing, in my life in Rio, that was
so absorbing that I didn't even find time to write my
own people? Having fun, carousing, enjoying life, no
doubt! Had I already managed to catch a navy officer,
or an aviator who would be less dense? She would not
forget me in her prayers and would be waiting for me
to come home soon, especially in view of the informa-
tion that she was giving me at the beginning of the
letter—

Scribbled on the edge of the sheet: "Glória gave birth
to a son. He is fat, weighed nine pounds at birth, has
dark eyes, and looks like his father. You will get the announcement by regular mail."

The next day we had lunch together downtown.

Never had I seen Isaac so happy, so close to me.

He didn't allude to anything that had happened the previous evening, he didn't ask for any promises, but in a firm and natural way he showed that I was his. He helped me with my coat when I came in, held my hand in plain sight at the table, ordered for me, once straightened a lock of my hair that came unpinned.

He got me to talk, and smilingly asked me to tell him about myself, other men, other occasions. And I told him about my few innocent little romances, and Maria José's, with boys from the high school, our carnival flirtations, our quick conversations on streetcars en route to the office. I said little about Aluísio, however, and nothing at all about Raul. Why bring them into it? No use digging up old corpses. Or new ones either, of course.

Isaac had picked out a curious menu, full of raw greens that were vile and tasted of sand. And he laughed at my barbarian ways, because I wanted to throw on the floor some reddish roots that tasted like leaves.

Here I am speaking only of him, for I myself was nothing. A plaything, a sweetheart, a child, I responded only to the touch of his hands, in my special state of euphoria: I would laugh and tell him things, eat, drink the purple wine, and click my teeth on the wineglass, deriving all my happiness from that state of joyful passivity. I saw nothing of the movement of the streets, I did not recognize my few acquaintances, I could see only him—his mouth, his blue eyes, his large white hands, which, accomplices of the dark and of any chance encounter, kept seeking me, touching me.

Upon leaving our small café, on the corner near the skyscraper, he took me to the Library. He had me sit down in an unobtrusive spot and gave me a book:

"I must study, Guta. Stay here and read. I don't want you out on the streets. If I get to thinking that you're walking around out there, I'll drop everything and run after you—"

He sat down at the nearest table, spread out his tablets on top of the books he was studying. And I sat watching him, the volume he had given me unopened in my hand.

I saw him as he sat, indolently bending over the table, his large lanky body in repose. And he seemed to me incomparably handsome. How does one create, how does one form, that marvel of flesh and sinew—a man? The hand as it writes, the torso that takes shape as it leans back in the chair, the curve of the nape of the neck, the vigorous line of the jaw—how perfect all this is, how serene and full of power and beauty! I was not seeing him, my Isaac, at that moment; I was seeing man, the human creature, the miracle of living beings, set there before my eyes, awakened and interested through the power of love. He did not look at me and was not even thinking of me, absorbed as he was in his notes. And I pondered all the potential riches stored in that body, evil and good, tenderness, anger, caresses, capacity for love. From his serene and concentrating features, I sought to reconstruct his expression in moments of love; it seemed to me that this was not the same man as yesterday's, and that it was impossible to find one within the other.

Who was that man I now saw? A stranger, no more than a stranger. A person needs but to closet himself with his thoughts to set up between himself and all others a complete frontier zone, with soldiers, borders, and an unknown sea in the middle. We had been going together for so many days, his face was already as familiar as the ring on my finger; I could even draw it from memory. However, I did not recognize it now, perhaps because his face was different, and we have a special look for each sentiment and each sensation.

I quickly began to feel lonesome and abandoned in the midst of so many books, so many strange silent people, each concerned with his own reading, holding in my own hand a volume whose name I could scarcely make out, and whose contents were unknown to me, as was everything else there.

But Isaac took his eyes off his notes and smiled at me —and suddenly I had him back, and with him my own resources.

It was evident that Isaac was in love with me, but he had never spoken to me of love. He made no plans, sought no promises, took no mortgages on the future. In moments of most intimate tenderness, or in others of no importance, his words were always appropriate only to the sentiment at hand, the sensation of the moment.

And I, who did my dreaming and planning all by myself, never dared ask for a thing, imitating his neglect; I saw the day of leaving draw close and still kept silent, afraid to break the charm, afraid of disappointing him, of making him think me capable of some sort of design or scheme with my heart. I took pride precisely in the gesture of giving myself without asking in return, or at least without showing that I expected anything.

There was nothing left of myself that I might not have given him, either of heart or body. And he had accepted all, gravely moved, but without any great display of gratitude, without meekness or remorse, without any thought of owing me anything.

It was as if I had been his wife for a great while, and my surrender, which meanwhile cost me in tears, in terrible, secret repentance, had for him no other meaning beyond its own immediate content of pleasure and tenderness.

When he took me, he asked for nothing, accompanying his own desire gradually, inducing me to share it, smiling at my fears and hesitations, obstinately, gently, inflexibly.

Rather than of physical pain, that first surrender left me with a sensation of fear and of secret humiliation; the pleasure that he got from me was so much his alone, so separate from me, diminished me so much, that I didn't feel any of the mysterious pleasure whose approach made him gasp as if suffering, and which afterward left him somnolent and quiet, sprawled on the sand, in a kind of happy unconsciousness, with his face nestled against my breast.

I was lucid, lucid and deeply hurt, and extraordinarily sad and apprehensive. I wished for him to console me, to embrace me, to make up to me for everything. But Isaac, in his torpor, left me to myself, and it looked as though my function had ended there—at least until his desire revived.

The cold wind on the beach chilled my hands, I

rolled up in my coat, shivering. Sand was filling my hair, and a fine salty dust, raised by the wind, was lashing my face.

Isaac, awake at last, turned to me, took me in his arms. "You look like you're freezing to death!"

I huddled closer, hugged him desperately in my arms. "Yes, Isaac. And I've been thinking—"

His eyes, wide open now, were so close that I could feel his lashes brush my face.

As simply as possible I summed up my vague fears: "And—have you ever thought about—what if I should have a baby?"

He kissed me first, almost took my breath away, and then stretched out again and laughed, looking up at the stars: "He sure would be some kid!"

I said nothing more and continued thinking, trying to fathom the reason for his laugh and what his feelings might be, whether tenderness for his possible child and love for me—or indifference, inattentiveness, levity.

I never found out for sure. And I never understood his heart, not that day, nor any other. I don't know whether I was for Isaac just one more girl, that he took with a certain tender pity, or whether he considered me truly a woman, at that instant the only one, the beloved, the chosen.

Can it be that I had in his life the same explicit and inextinguishable meaning that he had in mine?

I never learned.

Furthermore, even today, what do I know about love? What is a man's attitude toward each woman he possesses? What difference does he possibly establish between one act of possession and another?

He may at times say to each a particular word of

heartfelt intimacy that touches her profoundly and would induce her to give him more, if there were more to give. May such a word not be a commonplace of the occasion, something trite and deformed by use, just as mechanical as other amorous attitudes? Any phrase of common courtesy, if heard with the heart, might have a very rich and deep meaning. Meanwhile, it goes its way, without awakening either interest or gratitude, without involving any real commitment, mere formality that it is. Perhaps men use love's tenderness as they use their "pleased to meet you," on the street. And it is woman's ingenuousness and inexperience that see confessions and avowals in what is nothing more than an ordinary courtesy.

The happy abandon at the end, the pulsing fever just before, the incoherent, touching cries—these are perhaps dictated by the satisfied flesh, not by the loving heart.

Or is it both that speak? Was it both that spoke through Isaac, his flesh and his heart?

My best moments, or what might have been my best, were ruined by that kind of musing. Only when Isaac was not in my presence was I capable of loving him, and then, and only then, everything seemed to me complete and marvelous.

When I was with Isaac, it always seemed to me that he was letting me down or running away from me.

And in the final days we had only one moment of absolute identification: when I threw myself into his arms on the evening of my departure, during our private leave-taking, before the official good-byes in the presence of everyone.

With my head on his shoulder, I was sobbing. And he took my chin in hand, turned my face upward, and stood looking at me for a long time. His eyes were full of tears and his lips were trembling. Then he buried his face in my hair, choking back his emotion. Finally he murmured:

"And what hurts me is not to be able to keep you with me, not to be able to demand that you stay—"

I made no reply. If he had asked me to stay, I would certainly have obeyed, belonging to him as I did. But he himself was the one who did not even face the possibility of seeing me stay and alluded to it as to something impossible.

I wiped my eyes, smiled, caressed his face, his hair, with my unsteady fingers:

"One of these days you will come and get me. Or else in a year from now I'll be back. Don't ever move from your house and wait for me—"

From the living room the Major was calling, and Dona Alice was walking back and forth nervously. I pulled away from Isaac, who still attempted to hold me back and kept frantically kissing my arms, my fingers that were evading him. Feverishly, I left the room, dazed, faint from shedding tears that blinded my eyes like a flame.

I didn't look back at the city; mechanically I took leave of my friends, of the noisy band of fellows from the pension who took me to the pier.

The ship pulled away slowly, as if it were swimming

with human hands, the weak and halting hands of an old man. Only a half meter of ocean separated us, and Isaac was already lost to me, lost, lost! Two more fathoms of dark oily water, and I could still see his eyes, and his wonderful everyday smile. Very, very gradually, with a cruel, measured slowness, things got smaller and smaller, and more and more indistinct, until finally even his dark shape faded into the gray of the pier, into the motionless mass of the city.

I ran to the stateroom and tumbled into my bunk, still clutching tight against my coat the book he had brought me for my going-away.

When I went back on deck, the city could no longer be seen, just a faint, ill-defined, blackish line of distant land.

I stayed there until nightfall, sitting in a deck chair, all alone, with no desire to concern myself with the pilots, the young ladies, and the four big jovial soccer players in wool pull-overs, sitting next to me. A call bell rang. The girls went shrieking down the stairs, the players made a circle around me and waited a while, then slowly went their way.

I leaned on the rail and stood there looking at the water. Underneath the ship, the bottomless abyss, at that somber hour devoid of form and color. And it made your head spin and your flesh crawl to imagine the terrible and deadly mysteries, the icy vortex, that lay hidden in those waters so nearby, beneath the frothy layer of foam.

Overhead the cloudless and moonless sky was as blue and somber as the sea, and equally close and distant, equally unfathomable.

The bell rang again, I went downstairs and sat down at table with the others.

The girls continued their laughing, the pilots were alternately grave and roistering. The ship was a little iron shell, trailing smoke and hurrying over the top of hundreds of meters of deep, dark, cold, treacherous water. But inside it everyone was eating and laughing, carefree and joyful. Any insignificant little fish in that ocean was bigger, stronger, swam better; and it could move about freely and safely in that realm, which was for us sheer terror and death. Still, fish were of no importance, they were born and they died as if they grew out of the water and later dissolved into the water, as transitory and numberless as the waves breaking on the shore. We, meanwhile, weak, small, pusillanimous, we were men, each one doggedly conscious of his importance and his individuality; we identified each other, sought each other over miles and miles of earth and sea; we loved a unique object, a tiny unit of humanity, marked by a name, bound inflexibly to laws and duties of remote and debatable origin.

And there are so many men, so many fish, the sea is so vast, the tiny vessel rushes to such a far-off place—

The obsequious traveler opposite me began to dance and weave through the fine mesh of tears that were blurring my eyes. His words buzzed in my ears, became confused with the sound of the orchestra, gave me a headache. I gently pushed away the glass of bottled water that he had set before me, got up, said I felt unwell, and went to my stateroom to cry.

I got back, took over my job, returned to the monotony of signing the office log, went back to sharing the room with Maria José, and to watching on Saturdays the well-to-do funeral processions that passed by. I introduced some modifications on my side of the room. From Rio I had brought several reproductions of paintings by Picasso, by Corot, and the "Tehura" by Gauguin, that had been clipped out of numbers of *Vogue*, which Dona Alice bought because of the fashion plates. I lined up new books on the book shelf, volumes with yellow covers that spoke to me of Isaac and of minutes dreamed about and lost. But I didn't read them much, worked absent-mindedly at the office, no longer caught the streetcar with a gang of office mates, wept frequently; it was as if I were out of my element and forced to become a part of a world that I'd escaped from. I felt as if I had been obliged to return to my childhood, to skip rope, to tell my beads at midday with the Sisters.

And I was extremely worried for fear I was going to have a baby.

The thought of it never left me. At home in our room, long after the lights had been put out, when Maria José, at my side, would be snoring softly, I would be thinking: what would she say, what a shock, what a scandal! I had told her about Isaac as a sweetheart, perhaps even fiancé, without having the courage to tell her the truth, to tell her how far along things had gotten.

On the streetcar, sitting with the other girls from the office, I would laugh to myself, thinking bitterly: if they only knew, if the boys should guess, if they should even dream!

And my heart was an aching confusion of things bad

and good, cowardly and heroic. I dwelt in fear of op-
posing everyone, of Godmother's dramatic and official
malediction, of Papa's dismayed surprise, of giving up
my job—of everything that was brutally and pitilessly
going to crash down on top of me.

I wasn't counting on Isaac. I had never asked him for
anything, he had promised me nothing; everything between us was distant and interrupted.

And I felt tenderness, curiosity, excitement, a virgin's
curiosity, which can only be fully satisfied after maternity and which bring about consequences, which she,
as a virgin, is not willing to accept. I started thinking
about the child, about this child of mine who was still
only a threatening possibility, who might shortly be a
warm and living thing inside me: what would it be like
to feel his tiny hands touching my breast, to sleep with
this precious weight in my arms?

A child, always calling me, needing me, without
Isaac's detachment, without his offhanded affection—
a child who would never dispense with me, could not
do without me, would never leave me.

And thinking of it, I usually lost my fear.

Jandira's aunt died, the little old lady who had embraced her and wept on her wedding day. She left her
a house and some money in the bank.

Maria José and I went to visit Jandira, to give her our
condolences, and to talk over old times. The town is so

tiny, and people drop out of sight so easily! I don't know how long it had been since we had seen her, since the days of the imposing old mansion on Guajeru Street.

There seems to be only enough of life for each of us to look after himself and to let his eyes rove vacantly over the faces of those who are nearest. A different district, a distant street, and you're already in another world. And no one has time for explorations in those faraway lands.

This is, at any rate, the explanation I give myself and that I would attempt to give Jandira, as I invented reasons for our not getting together. She, of course, always the same, rushed up and hugged us, and began talking about herself, frankly, affectionately, naturally, as in the Colégio days.

She looked happy, despite being in mourning. Happy and calm, defying the world as usual, but defying it now without her former dark despair.

Into her life had come a measure of joy and recompense: she had a lover. She told us everything, perhaps to justify herself: she told what she had hidden from us in that last visit—her unhappy life with her husband, his degradation, the penury in which she lived, her slaving away at her machine night and day to assure milk for her child.

The inheritance came, bringing with it salvation. It was going to give her security and rescue her from her excessive labors. It was high time: she could feel her kidneys worn out with so much bending over the machine, and her blind child might not be able to survive his general wretchedness and the lack of medicines much longer. And now Jandira was hoping to be able to live, hoping to get some of the good things out of life that had always been denied her.

The other man had been a friend of her husband's, worked in the same ancient calling, was generous and good, and was her support, her joy, her way of getting redress.

Maria José was amazed and speechless at her confession. If only her ears had never heard!

Jandira laughed, serenely, and she understood the other's astonishment, understood and faced up to everything as always. Perhaps there was a little taste of victory in it for her.

For my part, I supported her. She squeezed my hand, and whispered:

"I knew it, Guta. I knew you would understand me. And I shouldn't have said anything in front of Maria José."

Maria José looked down, concurring softly:

"True—I'd prefer not to know."

Jandira took us to see her little boy. He had grown; he no longer spent the whole day in his hammock, but stayed in a little yard beside the house, stroking a leaf of caladium with his tiny hand, or sitting on the veranda steps with a cat in his lap, singing for hours on end.

His baby voice is plaintive and monotonous. It reminds you of a blind beggar's voice, one of those with violin and gourd. He makes children's songs sound like the "Lord bless you's" the beggars sing. He started singing, after we went in, as soon as Jandira asked him:

"Sing, my son. Sing for Aunty Guta and Aunty Josie to hear."

For a long time I sat on the veranda step with him, listening, feeling the same attraction I had felt the other time I had seen him in his hammock, counting his tiny fingers, so quietly.

I was afraid I was going to weep, but, held by the blind child's strange fascination, I didn't want to go away. No wonder he fascinated me: aren't there primitive peoples who even worship these tiny innocent creatures, blind or insane, resembling inhabitants of another world, seers of mysterious vistas inaccessible to us?

And I was also held by the thought of the child who was perhaps developing inside me, and who, unfortunately, might also be blind and sing, and be sad and ill-fated.

The little fellow didn't talk to us. It was evident that he was not interested in anyone but his mother and his cat.

The two of them were for him his plaything, his company, the surrounding warmth of life, the hand that feeds, the mouth that kisses, the voice that soothes. The rest didn't matter, didn't even exist.

ISAAC'S LETTER

"Guta, *man taire, man ketsele, man tzigale,* I wish I could write you in my own language. It is too hard for me to express what I feel for you if I must study it beforehand. I appear to be lying when I say things that I must translate first; they don't emerge naked from my heart as I want them to, naked and spontaneous as when they were born; they become deformed and grow old as they pass through the grammar and the dictionary.

"Even those sweet names I called you at the beginning, which are words of love among my people, would perhaps seem funny to you if I should translate them here: 'My beloved, my kitten, my lamb.'

"Why did you go away? I never consented to it, and the truth is that you never asked me. Who gave you the right to abandon me?

"I study little and badly, I am a poor wretched Jew, in a threadbare coat, an extinguished cigarette in hand, spending almost every afternoon gloomily seated on a park bench. I think about the girl from far away who came here unexpectedly, who let me love her those cold nights at the beach—about my girl whom the sea gave me and then later took away.

"I go in the café, and go right out, because there's nothing in there any more. Nor is there anything any longer for me in books, nor anything in my phonograph records.

"At times I go out to Arpoador Beach and sit down in the place we used to sit. But everything is fierce and solitary there, the sea, the night, the rocks; and my yearning for you, which I feel like a weight inside me, is as hard and motionless and insoluble as a rock.

"What is your life like there, so far away from me? How was the ocean voyage? Your letters tell me nothing. I hope you have not consented to listen to the sentimental drivel of some ship's officer, leaning on the guardrail, gazing up at heaven or at the ship's foamy wake, and sighing. I had a thousand times rather you stayed in your stateroom nauseated.

"Here everyone speaks your name and it irritates

me. It's intolerable for so many to know you, for so many to feel that they have a right to your friendship, to memories of you.

"The Major, mainly. The other day he told me you reminded him of Joan of Arc. Who knows why? (Do you recall Villon's poem about 'Jehanne, la bonne Lorraine'? Once we read it together at the Library.)

"Speaking of verses, today I am sending you a little volume by André Spire, a poor yid like myself, small and lonely, full of secret sadness.

"And before I say good-bye, let me tell you as he tells the children, in a poem that I ask you to read soon: 'Il y a trop de baisers pas donnés entre nous—'

"P.S. My matter with the Immigration Service is getting worse by the day. You know I entered the country with a tourist's passport, which has now expired but which I have managed to keep getting extended. Everything now depends on the validation of my diploma. There are exams to be taken, and this has always frightened me. I don't know what I shall do. I am afraid of being made to leave.

"P.P.S. Where are all the women of this world? Where have they gone? I can't see a single one."

Maria José was praying. She was engaged in her favorite spiritual exercise, the meditations on the Passion. From time to time she would take the crucifix in her hands and kiss one of the wounds of the image. The Christ was of plaster of Paris, incarnate in violent colors, with large tears of blood flecking the body, golden curls, and flowery purple shadows under the eyes. He didn't seem dead, in the midst of so many colors. Maria José, however, saw him dead, saw the tragedy, and wept and beat her breast.

Is it possible that she was really moved, really suffering, simply through the mental, almost literary, evocation of that faraway drama?

What is pity, what is charity, what is love of one's fellowman? What is it about another's pain that pains us, what impression do the sufferings of others actually make on us?

For my own part, I think that they matter to us only when they assume a direct, immediate, physical quality —when they can be seen.

Faced with the open wound of some poor devil, something, perhaps my stomach, turns upside down within me; one feels the physical ills of another, suffers with him. However, even that must be very brutal, very visible, in order to make a profound impression. Basically, other people's hunger is an abstract idea. And abstract ideas reach the intelligence, but they do not easily stir the emotions. People have to *see* hunger, have to *feel* hunger.

Why was Maria José crying? Where did she get the tragic inspiration for those tears? From the death of God, who so quickly rose again in glory, and all that two thousand years ago?

(Only that which makes us suffer really has any significance as evil for us. Because, in reality, only I am important to myself; only we have validity for ourselves. We understand others' suffering, we understand "with our flesh" only when we ourselves are to some degree touched by it.)

After all is said and done, what is evil, what is good, what is love of one's fellowman?

I waited for Maria José to finish her long prayer and tried to convey my impressions to her.

She shook her head in discouragement:

"Aluísio was right when he used to say that you are a force of nature. Like a rock, like an animal. What do you expect to gain thinking about such matters? What indeed can you understand by 'soul' and by 'God'? That's why you throw yourself at men, without remorse or fear [I had already told her a few more things about my friendship with Isaac]. That's why you approve of Jandira's madness. You have no notion of good or evil."

And what about her? Who pointed out good and evil for her? What did she know about it, especially about evil, poor thing who hadn't done any more in this world than wear out her knees praying, and tire out her voice teaching?

"It's all in what you think. We carry evil around in our heart, Guta. People instinctively desire evil. And furthermore, everything around us is so filthy. I don't know what would become of me if it weren't for religion holding me in check. I think I'd be lost, that I'd start sinning like mad. I'm full of desire and terribly afraid."

I stood looking at Maria José. Why was she setting those outer boundaries? How was it she knew them so well?

I, for my part, no longer knew what a good or an evil thought might be. My recollections of Isaac for example? They would perhaps be sinful for Maria José.

I on the other hand was moved to tenderness just to think back on our short-lived happiness. And I should never bring myself to consider my memory of Isaac an evil thought.

"When I think about my father and the kind of life he leads, I lose hours of sleep. I feel like giving up everything to take a chance and try out that sort of life. To challenge the world as he did, to sink to the bottom, to end it all. At times I am afraid of myself. What is pleasure like, what is that other life like, Guta? What I do know is that every pleasure is a sin."

As for me, I no longer had that kind of dream. What is there to know about? Men in the throes of passion. No, I don't dream about that any more. Perhaps I still wish—wish for certain experiences. For the rest, I exhausted all my curiosity, I got disillusioned in a hurry.

Pleasure—my mind immediately turns to Raul's hot, sweaty hands, to the wretched little automobile, skidding in the mud, wildly digging its own ruts, while I sat fearful and anxious to get away.

And Raul is one of those who represent "the world," the world that terrifies and seduces Maria José with its diabolical, prohibited attractions. He has his legend of wayward women, his Bohemian way of life, the luster of his canvases and colors, the frail, romantic figure of an artist.

But for me, after seeing him at such close range, I can think only of his tremulous way of speaking, his Adam's apple continually moving, his quivering nostril—a small thin body that was famished and supplicating, miserable. How humbly he implored, and in his frenzy how childish, despicable, and low!

Lost in meditation, Maria José had grown very still.

Finally, she uttered a mighty sigh, knelt once more, put her head between her hands, and placed herself in contact again with the other world.

Likewise silent, I contemplated her thoughtfully from my bed. Only a meter of floor separated us. Brought up together, living together, identified in our likes and dislikes, we were, nevertheless, like two women of different nations and of different tongues. Not even that, because Isaac and I were of different nations and of different tongues, yet we understood each other. It's true that I was in love with him.

I stuck out my hand, found the switch, turned off the light. I went quickly to sleep, finding no sins to think about. I woke up later and was startled by a form bending near Maria José's bed. It was she, still in prayer, punishing herself, of course, for the terrible pleasures her heart desired, for the evil thoughts she persisted in having.

As if they even existed, Maria José. As if bad things were simply bad—without poetry or beauty. Even your father's great sin—is it really a sin? You look upon him as a reprobate, and you weep and pray for him. He lives as best he can. Why do you judge him? Who knows, in this world, where the sinful are? Who knows if the sinful even exist?

And nevertheless she finds nothing wrong in misery, sickness, and inequality. She didn't become indignant when she went with me to the Charity Hospital and saw the sick rotting in their beds, foul-smelling, with bloated stomachs, skeletal hands, the green skin of the dead.

Maria José thinks it all right for a dog catcher's wagon to operate. She thinks it all right for Dona Júlia to beat the little colored girl who delivers the lunch pails. After all, who ever taught her what evil is?

Can evil be that which gives the impression of being wrong? For example: the dog catcher's wagon that I've just mentioned. The stories of war: fine-looking young men who die disemboweled by bayonets, who are cut to pieces by shrapnel.

In a cinema newsreel the other day I saw the bombardment of a Chinese city. The camera showed a section of a street, near a door. A bomb had fallen, everyone was running, and one saw only legs in motion, legs in mad flight. Sitting on a doorstep, an abandoned child was crying. People kept passing by, no one heard him; he howled with fright, stuck his tiny hands in his mouth, began crying again, turning his head and his eyes in all directions, toward all those who ran by without seeing him.

He had been hit on the head, perhaps couldn't walk yet, and in his small heart there must have been con centrated at that moment all the terror in the world. All alone in the midst of the bombs, the destruction, motherless, friendless, forgotten.

Poor little Chinese boy—dramatically opening wide his arms, trying to grasp the legs of those running by. I wonder who came to his aid? Not the photographer, loaded down with his equipment, occupied in taking other pictures. Who then stopped for him, touched by the injuries, the blind despair of this abandoned child?

At Glória's house we recalled friends we'd lost track of. We spoke of Violeta, who had become a prostitute, and the others started coming to mind:

"Granny" Aurinívea: her voice was hoarse and faint; she was as sweet and patient as a little old lady. She went on to become a Sister and is even consumptive, they say.

Aurinha: curly hair, pimply face, head-strong, romantic, ungovernable imagination. She would talk only about things that were strange and inaccessible, the Foreign Legion, hara-kiri, Alpine convents amid eternal snows, the lepers of the Middle Ages. She too went on to become a nun. What else, if not the divine, could give her her impossible worlds? She received her habit from the Mother House in Paris, and from there went to a mission in Indo-China. Perhaps her dream came true; I think, however, that she is already disillusioned with washing and catechizing dirty obstinate little Chinese children. Or perhaps now she's dreaming of something else. Asia must be rich in mirages.

Marília: Marília, so easygoing, plain, and good, with her look of calm assurance and inner wealth of tenderness and passionate impulses. Hardly out of the Colégio, she fell in love and married a young fellow with a moustache and sideburns, the juvenile leading man of the neighborhood theatrical group. She died of typhus, two months after giving birth to a daughter.

I went to see her at the private hospital. She was dying and didn't realize it, would hold hands with her husband, and ask, her speech already made difficult by approaching death—"Walter, did they starch your white suit?"

The widower got married again, to a slender, pretty

girl, with platinum hair. The baby girl is homely and sad-looking, just like Marília, and has inherited her impassioned nature. The child adores her stepmother, who is desperate to make her look prettier, puts big red bows in her hair, dresses her in embroidery and lace booties. I met them in the street the other day. The stepmother was walking along rapidly in a cloud of perfume, the little one trotting along behind, dazzled and out of breath, without ever taking her eyes off the blond figure who was pulling her along. And in her small tender eyes, I seemed to see the same expression as in her mother's when she lay dying.

These were the things we talked about in Glória's bedroom. I was cradling her child in my arms, and its sweet baby's breath warmed my breast. Just looking at it, holding it thus in my arms, I felt calm and happy, full of hope and affection, oblivious of all my worries, as though I were being solaced before my time. How good he smelled, how soft and pink! Prettier than a flower, than a fruit, than the prettiest and simplest things.

Glória pretended to listen to Maria José, but she didn't take her eyes off me and her son. Perhaps she was jealous of the happy feeling that the little boy's presence gave me; or perhaps, as in the old days of her love affair, she wished to share with me the excessive weight of tenderness that oppressed her.

Suddenly the little one awakened, started to yell furiously, as if I had cockleburs in my lap, or as if my hands were hurting him.

This moment belonged to him. Glória opened her kimono, held out her arms toward me. I handed her the little boy and it broke my heart. I had an absurd desire to weep, as if I were handing over all my hopes, my happiness, my consolation.

I got sick. I was feverish, delirious, and had terrible pains.

Dona Júlia was the person taking care of me, who put the ice pack on my stomach, who gave me the steaming bitter tea, who changed my bedclothes now and then.

I think she understood everything. That's why she didn't call the doctor. That's why she kept Maria José away from the room and, silently, watchfully, moved in to join me.

On the day the pains were at their height, when I was hanging on in her arms, frantically groaning and asking to die, she said to me, sadly:

"Baby, baby, what did you do?"

But this was her only recrimination. Never again did she ask me a thing, nor did she criticize. Sometimes she just stood looking at me; but when she saw that I had noticed and was also looking at her, she turned her head away, inventing an excuse, and silently wiped her eyes on her coat sleeve.

One night I was crying inconsolably, my head buried in the pillow, my sobs completely convulsing me.

Dona Júlia came in the room, softly approached the bed. For a long time she stroked my hair, without saying a word. Finally, she whispered:

"I'm sorry, dear. You're not to blame for not having a mother."

Maria José, who also perhaps suspected something, seemed to be avoiding me. She came in from outside, came quickly into the room, laid her hand on my forehead or gave me a fleeting kiss; she offered as a pretext a novena at the Cathedral, or a catechism class, and went away.

I believe she feared an explanation between us, feared the awful things she preferred not to know.

The world is so dirty and sad! Why know about everything? What about poor Guta, oh my Lord? When will she be well again? Let it be soon, and let her change her ways and get some sense in her head! Oh my sweet Our Lady, why didn't you take better care of her?

Had I had some secret intention when I let myself be hauled away by Maria José to the amusement park? Since the evening before I had been feeling ill, with dull pains here and there, dizziness, malaise, whose source I really couldn't identify.

But I said nothing and went with her; I put on very heavy make-up and with paint covered up the purplish circles under my eyes, my deathly pale cheeks.

The giant Ferris wheel turned slowly and made you afraid, so afraid! It would stop at the top, the little seats rocking back and forth like fruit up in the air; I started getting dizzy, thought I was going to fall out, and the fright was so great that it gave me a pain in the pit of my stomach.

Then I spun crazily around on the "whip," collided furiously in the little automobiles on the race track. With each crash I felt something hurt me inside, something heavy and sharp.

I should have stopped. I wanted to raise my voice and ask them to stop it. But I didn't dare; I just let myself stay, and put myself in the hands of whatever destiny had wished to bring me there.

Maria José was like a child, her hair blowing in the wind, laughing, shouting my name.

The whip, on one of its curves, came close to the bar. As we passed by it, I heard a drunk indignantly shouting: "That's a crime!"

Startled, I shrank back into my seat.

A crime? If it were a crime, would Maria José be calling to me like that, so innocently, so happily?

And I kept going, rode again, laughed with her, let myself be dragged madly along, only shutting my eyes at the more violent shocks, which shook me all over.

At certain moments I would rouse, want to jump out, save myself, get away from there. But my next thought was that I was doing nothing, taking no action, just letting myself be carried along by the will of others. That was no crime. The drunk had gone away, gesticulating violently between two brutish Germans who were dragging him outside.

The poor little one went away forever. Who can say whether he would not have had the same blue eyes as Isaac?

He never even reached the point of having eyes—

I'm going home, back to the *sertão*. Night is just about to fall; the train speeds between indistinct masses that I don't recognize, where I make out houses, trees, perhaps the shadows of small mountains.

I feel more and more sad, ill, and alone. In the seat next to me a fleshy, noisy young woman is traveling with a child on her lap. Opposite is her husband, with the older child beside him. I try to escape their invading intimacy; I become absorbed in the window, in the landscape being swallowed up by the twilight.

The couple talk, make plans, at times disagree in a low voice; the girl stops and looks for a long time at my pale, scrawny hands, with Mama's little ring that keeps slipping down my finger, my face melancholy and drained of color, all of me tired and sickly.

The heavy air of the train is suffocating and smells foul. The children are crying now and press close to their mother.

My head aches, my heart aches, everything aches. I think about Isaac. How much land and sea and humanity separating us! I have the feeling I can still see his hands, still hear his laugh, his strange grave way of talking. What can he be doing, so far from me, in his so distant land, as the train plunges into the *sertão?* Every second means the advance of a few more meters of track, and the loss of one more probability of ever seeing him again. Whom will he ever play his records for? In my purse I have his four letters. How dead they are, now, inexpressive and empty! What good are written words? They are worth less than any kind of spoken word, than all the beloved words that the sea wind carried away. What good does it do to keep old letters? I can't hang on to the kisses he gave me.

The train advances into the *sertão*, into the night that

is my escape route. And I go with it, go within it, am part of it. Isaac is far away, so far away that I can't really imagine where he is, without having confused visions of maps and scales of distances. So far away that no familiar image is sufficient to represent that distance to me, and I must think in numbers.

Now, each of us has returned to his own milieu, each is reintegrated in his own landscape, and is more completely lost from the other. And there were moments when he was so close, his face so close to mine that I could no longer see it, as if he had already become a part of me.

There was a moment when everything seemed to us shared, equal, and, especially, immutable. We seemed to have risen above all things, the seas, distance, nationality, language, for that fatal and definitive meeting, guided by a sure and secret destiny that had arranged our coming together.

Everything seemed accomplished and complete. He did not wish to think of the future—I didn't dare.

And, after all, it had been only for a moment. And that moment had passed. Each has now resumed being what he was before, and, certainly, we shall never see each other again.

The train is loafing along, behind schedule. Night has closed in completely, ashen and melancholy, like the arid brush country from which it arises.

I flee from my seat, go through the corridor, reach the platform at the end of the car, which is the last one.

The roadbed comes up from the shadows, as if it were suddenly born out of the nearby horizon, between the trees and the limpid sky that is cloudless, moonless, with only its stars.

I look at the Three Marias, all together, shining. Glória sparkles, impassively, with a steady blue gleam. Maria José, the little one, burns with a twinkle, modest and restless as always. And I—I also shine, and difficult as it will be, will still shine for a while—and my light seems to have a moist and ardent brilliance of eyes that weep.

And I've no idea how much longer I shall be there, lonely and forsaken, shining in the dark, until my light goes out.